TIME→ JUMP

Timothy J. Bradley

S0-CFY-998

This is a work of fiction. Names, characters, places, and incidents are either products of the author's imagination or, if real, are used fictitiously.

© 2015 Argosy Press
All rights reserved. No part of this book may be reproduced, transmitted, or stored in an information retrieval system in any form or by any means, graphic, electronic, or mechanical, including photocopying, taping, and recording, without prior written permission from the publisher.
First paperback edition

Library of Congress Cataloging-in-Publication Data

Bradley, Timothy J.
  Time jump / by Timothy J. Bradley.—First paperback edition.
     pages cm.—Sci Hi; 3)
  Summary: "When Sci Hi's school for whiz kids is blasted 400 million years into the past, Paleontology class gets way more real—and way more lethal. To jump forward through time, Sidney, Hari, and Penny must survive slimy trilobites, paleo sharks, and hungry dinos"—provided by publisher.
  ISBN 978-1-4807-4215-4 (pbk. : alk. paper)
  ISBN 978-1-4807-4217-8 (hardcover : alk. paper)
  ISBN 978-1-4333-8981-8 (ebook : alk.paper)
[1. High schools--Fiction. 2. Schools--Fiction. 3. Time travel—Fiction. 4. Dinosaurs—Fiction. 5. Prehistoric animals—Fiction.] I. Title.
  PZ7.B7258Ti 2014
  [Fic]—dc23
                          2014026697

        Argosy Press
        5301 Oceanus Drive
        Huntington Beach, California 92649
        An imprint of Teacher Created Materials

Argosy
Press

TIME→ JUMP

CHAPTER 1

"Fighters ready!" a voice called over Sidney Jamison's headphones. He quickly adjusted the headset over his curly, brown hair. "The Nanobot Death Match will begin in five seconds."

Sid's VR goggles lit up, and he could see what his nanobot saw: a canyon surrounded by a vast, rugged terrain. Through his nanobot's eyes, the canyon looked immense. But in reality, the canyon was just the size of a pinhead.

Sid drew in a deep breath. *It's battle time!*

The nanobot tournament was born when Sid realized the tiny machines used at Goddard Island might be good for something other than fabricating materials and conducting research on microsize devices. They could be modified and customized into outlandish configurations by bolting, welding, or sticking on destructive bits and pieces. Microsize mayhem was way more fun than delving into some boring assignment about ancient piles of dirt and bones.

When something sparked Sid's burning streak of curiosity, he worked through the night to find the answers to his questions. But he immediately dismissed anything that didn't trigger his curiosity as dull, dull, dull. The idea for the Nanobot Death Match came to Sid as he was procrastinating, looking for something—anything—to put off his Postmodern Paleontology project. *A bunch of stuff died*, he thought, *and that's basically it. What's the big deal? It's done and gone.* Sidney had always been more interested in the future than the past. He couldn't wait to find out what happened next, whether it was with technology, a scientific discovery, or lunch.

He had been killing time by setting up thousands of nanobots (too small to see without using a microscopic camera), in curving patterns on his desk, and then knocking them down like dominos. They all went down in sequence. Sid had spent hours that way.

But today, the line of knocked-over bots gave him a shot of inspiration. An idea exploded in his mind: *robot battles*! He turned suddenly in his chair. "Hey, Hari! Are you busy right now?"

Hari Gupta, Sid's roommate and friend, replied without turning around, "What do you think, Sid? I've been sitting here for hours trying to program a group of drill scanners so I don't wipe out traces of a meteor in 65-million-year-old rock."

"So, you're saying you're busy?"

Hari turned, annoyed. "*Yes*, Sid. I'm busy, and you should be, too. This project is a lot more work than I thought it would be. If you haven't started it, you'd better get to it."

Sid waved a hand dismissively. "I know, I know, but I just had a lethal idea. Check it out: nanobot battles! Wouldn't that be great?"

Sid watched as Hari tried not to smile. "It's not a bad idea. But I have to finish this project," he said. Hari turned back to his project.

Sid waited. He knew Hari wouldn't be able to resist.

A few seconds later Hari sighed and threw up his hands, "Aw, whatever. Let's do it!"

Sid and Hari spread the word through the Tesla dorm and beyond, and within a couple of hours, nearly every Sci Hi student had dropped his or her schoolwork and started preparing nanobots for battle. By dinnertime, Sid had set up a bracket system that pitted the four dorms against each other in a series of one-on-one battles.

Penny Day, Sid's other best friend, chided him in her clipped British accent, "I hope you realize what you've done. Not only are you procrastinating from working on your assignments, you've now convinced every other student to put off their work as well."

"Awesome, huh?" Sid grinned. "Hey, I'm not twisting anyone's arm. You don't have to take part in the tournament if you'd rather study, Penny."

Her dark eyes flashed. "Are you kidding? Pass up the chance to kick your butt—robotically speaking, of course? I wouldn't miss it."

The first battles were scheduled for the next day, after classes let out.

The Sci Hi staff knew something was up when they received an 800 percent increase in nanobot fabrication requests, but they made no attempt to stop the runaway bot production. *I never would have been able to pull this off at Bleaker High,* Sid marveled. *It's like they want us to mess up.*

Even Talos, an AI built by the scientists on Goddard Island, got in on the action. Talos was humanoid in shape, with a single blue eye lens on his face. Massive arms and legs were connected to his body with thick cables and shock absorbers. Even though he was a big, heavy machine, Talos moved precisely, giving him the appearance of a trained athlete. With his bulky body, Sid always thought of Talos as a "he." He had been programmed with a male-sounding voice, but lately the robotics department had been experimenting with accents, animal sounds, and even weird sound effects, like jet engines and thunder rumbles, to give the AI more personality. Sid had a soft spot for the intelligent machine. Talos had piloted the aircraft that brought Sid to Goddard Island, and he was the first to help Sid feel at home at Sci Hi.

"Hello, Sidney," Talos said in Sid's headphones. "Thank you very much for inviting me to be the announcer for the Nanobot Death Match. *Yeeeeeeeeeee!*" Sid jumped as a high-pitched screech flooded his ears. "That was a howler monkey call," Talos said.

That was *something*, Sid thought, but he simply said, "You're welcome, Talos" through gritted teeth. He unbuckled the antique watch that used to belong to his father and slipped it into his pocket so it wouldn't get damaged if he flung his arms around during the nanobot fight. "You might want to lower the volume when you're going to add a sound effect," Sid said. "Or at least warn everyone."

"I will," Talos said. "Are you ready to begin the match?"

"Yeah, go for it," Sid said. "Really put your heart into it...well, you know what I mean."

Talos's voice boomed in Sid's headphones. "*Ladieeeees and gentlemen*! Welcome to the Sci Hi Microdome Stadium, on beautiful Goddard Island, where the scientific meets the spectacular!"

Sidney laughed. Talos's latest voice implant made him sound less robotic, but he still didn't sound quite like a real human announcer. Perfect for a nanobot showdown!

Talos continued, "Tonight's bout features two combatants small in stature but *huuuuuge in heart*! In this corner, in blue and silver...TORRRRRRRNADOOOOO!" On the large image screen, a spotlight illuminated the nanobot. Cheers could be heard throughout the Tesla dorm. Tornado was thin and spindly, with rotor blades on its arms that could be used for hovering, defense, or all-out warfare. A student named Danny on the floor below had built it. Sid didn't know him that well, but he knew Danny was a major robotics nerd—and that was saying something at Sci Hi.

"In this corner, in green and orange...THE CRUSHERRRRRRRR!"

As the spotlight lit up Sid's combatant, he flexed his hands in the VR gloves and raised his arms overhead. His nanobot matched his moves at the microscopic level. Penny cheered behind him, watching the action on the huge wallscreen.

Sid was proud of The Crusher. He had modified his bot with leftover parts from a microelectronics assignment and used some tiny piezoelectric actuators he had borrowed from Hari's alarm clock. The design was based on a cartoon character he had liked as a kid, with a few additions. The Crusher had four short, stubby legs to give it stability. The bot's arms were thick cylinders that held cannonball-tipped pistons that could dent, crunch, or smash an opponent.

Sid didn't have much of a competitive streak, but he was definitely interested in building a fighting robot, even one that was microscopic. The actual fighting part would just be added fun. To Sidney's surprise, he had won matches against his first three opponents, and he was feeling confident going into this match against Tornado. *"Rotor blades? Ha!"* he thought. All he needed to do was catch Tornado and smash it into micro-junk. Simple.

He chose a track from Echo Chamber's latest album, and the pounding goth-pop beat filled his ears. *Yeah*, he thought, *"Piledriver" is the perfect song for this*.

Sidney quickly scanned the nanobot's systems on his goggle display. All systems go. As he flexed his fingers in the VR gloves, he saw the pistons fire and retract.

"Go get 'em, Sid!" Penny cried from behind him. Then, he heard Hari's footsteps approaching.

"Sorry I'm late," Hari said. "My alarm clock didn't go off, and it's seriously thrown off my schedule." Sid hunched down in his chair, hoping Hari wouldn't ask him about the missing actuators.

Shifting his focus back to the competition, Sid directed his bot into the canyon, switching to infrared so he could see into the shadows. If his nanobot were thrown outside the bright red circle surrounding it, he would lose the match. Suddenly, the view twisted crazily. Sidney found himself staring into the face of Tornado. The other nanobot had landed behind him and lifted The Crusher off the ground! Sidney stuck his arms out to the sides, rotating the bot's torso rapidly to escape. The Crusher's legs automatically telescoped outward as it fell, and Sid struggled to land it upright.

Maybe this wasn't going to be as easy as he had thought.

When Sid twisted the bot's torso, he spotted Tornado bearing down on him, rotor blades spinning. He brought The Crusher's arms up in defense, bending Tornado's rotor blades into useless scrap.

Yes! Sid thought. "Double-punch!" he yelled. He triggered the four cannonball-tipped pistons and started pounding on Tornado. Sid was able to push Tornado against a stalagmite as he sent a piston into the bot's large camera eyes, shattering both. He knocked the challenger to the ground, pinning it with the Crusher's piston arms.

Suddenly, the arena turned red. "Match over," Talos said. "Winner: The Crusher, piloted by Sidney Jamison!"

Sid pulled off his VR goggles and gloves as Hari and Penny clapped him on the back.

"Way to go, Sid!" Hari said.

"Well done, you!" Penny said. "But you know who your next match is with." She flashed a wicked grin, her dark eyes glinting like chips of obsidian. Unlike Sid, Penny was competitive. She was also tough and very smart. Penny would fight to win.

"Yup," Sid said nervously, strapping his dad's watch back on. "You."

"I hate to say it, but I think we need to put some time in on our Paleontology assignment," Hari said, leading them back to their rooms.

"Oh, come on," Sid groaned, shuffling after them. "There're a couple of bouts over in the Darwin dorm that I really want to watch."

"Hari's right," Penny chided, words and diagrams about the assignment scrolling on her dataglasses. "This is a big project, and we're going to need as much time as we can get."

"What's with you guys?" Sid said.

"Sorry, Sid," Hari said, sitting down at his desk. "We've goofed off enough for one day. Unlike you, we actually need to study to get good grades."

Sid sighed. "What was it we're supposed to be doing again? I tuned out when Dr. Petraglif was giving the assignment. Does she remind anyone else of a bird?"

"Don't be dense. You know we're studying mass extinctions," Penny said, ignoring the comparison. "We have to figure out what caused them in the past and whether we're going through one right now. What's with *you*? Usually, you can't wait to get geeky with us."

"I just don't get what the big deal is," Sid grumbled. "Lots of things have died, and we're here now, right? So what? I've got better things to do than study the past. There are robots to build and planets to explore."

"The big deal," Hari said patiently, "is that none of us would be here if it weren't for the dinosaurs getting wiped out."

"You're crazy," Sid said. "The dinosaurs were just too slow and stupid to get out of their own way, and then humans, with our awesome opposable thumbs, showed up and started building skyscrapers and space stations."

"Sorry, but you're the crazy one here," Penny said. "If that mass extinction hadn't happened and the dinosaurs hadn't become extinct, we wouldn't be here at all. With the dinos cleared away, there was room for new life to develop. Up until that point, mammals were just little furballs hiding from the larger predators. Once the dinosaurs were gone, mammals evolved into new forms and took over the planet."

"Well then, how can we be going through a mass extinction right now?" Sid argued. "Just look outside!" He turned on the image wall and located a channel that showed the view out over the ocean. "There are seagulls, pelicans, seals, dolphins, whales…all kinds of stuff! Plus, we haven't been hit by an asteroid. Put a check in the 'No Mass Extinction' box. Project finished."

"Wrong again, dope," Hari said. "Mass extinctions happen over geological lengths of time, like millions of years. They don't always need an asteroid, either."

"Climate change, volcanoes, disease, and gamma-ray bursts have all caused mass extinctions," Penny added. "Plants and animals are becoming extinct a thousand times faster than they did before humans existed! I'm actually focusing on that in my research."

"All right, enough! Let's just get this over with!" Sidney huffed as he pulled up the assignment on his voxpod.

When they entered the Postmodern Paleontology classroom the next day, Sidney, Penny, and Hari saw a large animal sitting on the laboratory table.

"Wow, nice!" Sid exclaimed. His friends nodded their agreement. The creature was nearly six feet long, with tiny arms and legs poking out from its sides, almost like a crocodile. Its head was wide and flat, with small eyes on top near the front of its snout. It was nearly submerged in a tank of water. Its skin was smooth and slick. When Sid bent closer to look at its small, dark eyes, one of them blinked.

Penny grabbed the back of Sidney's shirt and pulled him away as the animal began to open its huge mouth, revealing rows of small, sharp teeth as it hissed. With a shiver, Sid, Penny, and Hari quickly took their seats.

"I see you've met Fluffy," said Dr. Petraglif, their instructor, with a wink. She was small and thin, with spiky brown hair and bright green eyes. "He's a clone of *Metoposaurus*, a large amphibian that lived 220 million years ago, until a serious dry spell in what is now Poland produced a mass extinction. When amphibians like this big guy died out, other creatures, like modern-day alligators and crocodiles, were able to evolve to take over its ecological niche. We can see that progression through the fossil record.

"Fossils are like slices of time. When you add up all those slices, you learn a surprising amount of information about the creatures and their environment.

METOPOSAURUS

CARNIVOROUS

"Hmph," Sidney said, shaking his head.

Dr. Petraglif's head cocked slightly, and one sparkling eye fixed on him. "Did you have a comment, Sidney?"

Sidney cleared his throat nervously. "Well, I don't really get why those people spent so much time digging up old bones."

"Aren't you curious about the past? Just think about your own family. There's so much we can learn from our parents, grandparents, and all the generations that came before us. Following our curiosity to its natural conclusion leads us to embark on excavations like this. Fossils don't just tell us about extinct life forms. They tell us about the tree of life on Earth, and that includes humans. Fossils help us understand where our own species came from," Dr. Petraglif replied.

Sid knew something about the power of curiosity, but there was no way he could think about his own family tree without thinking about the big gap where his father should have been. Everything he knew about his dad was based on pictures and stories—tantalizing but mysterious razor-thin slices of time that told him about as much as some dusty old fossils might.

"With each fossil we uncover," Dr. Petraglif said with animation, "we learn more about our own past. Which brings me to our class project!" She directed the class's attention to the huge image wall at the front of the room.

It was a satellite view of a hilly, arid-looking landscape. "So far, we've been investigating what may have caused each of the five mass extinctions that decimated our planet in the past. Some more fringe scientists have suggested anaerobic bacteria may have produced large quantities of hydrogen sulfide, which would have been toxic to a wide variety of species and damaged the ozone layer. Others have suggested the rise of Pangea, the supercontinent, may have produced such dramatic changes in the weather and geography that species were not able to adapt in time. Perhaps the most popular proposal is the idea that a large asteroid caused the Permian-Triassic extinction. The impact of such a large chunk of rock colliding with Earth would have thrown tons of dust into the atmosphere, and tsunamis and firestorms may have damaged the land. The Earth's climate would have been altered for decades. But so far, no crater has been found. Without any hard evidence, it's hard to know which theory is correct.

"You've been assigned to test this theory and support it with historical evidence. Look for any signs in your investigating that could be tied to the possible sixth extinction that appears to be underway today. Now, it's time to get your hands dirty and start digging so you can test these hypotheses, at least virtually. I've secured time in the VR station for our class. Anyone who is interested can participate in a dig that's currently in progress in Mongolia. Who would like to sign up for a shift?"

Hari stared expectantly at Sidney until his hand joined the other students' in the air.

Sidney sighed. *Why didn't I sign up for Interplanetary Terraforming instead?* he wondered.

CHAPTER 2

Sid would never admit it, but the Mongolian fossil dig was pretty lethal. Reclining in one of the virtual reality labs in Sci Hi with powerful VR rigs over their heads and hands, the students were plugged into golf-cart-size dozerbots at a promising fossil site in Ulaanbaatar. The bots were easy to maneuver, and Sid was trying to do the tightest circles he could, raising clouds of dust with the dozer's spinning tires.

"Stop fooling around and help, please!" Penny said. "Hari and I are almost done planting our drillscanners. Hurry up, will you?"

"Yeah, Sid, let's go. Dr. Petraglif said the satellite is almost out of range, and they want to get the scans done in the next couple of hours," Hari chimed in. "You're holding everything up."

"Okay, okay!" Sid said. "Geez, you two are bossy. You remind me of my Housemate. That thing was always barking orders at me."

"You probably crashed the poor thing's chips," Penny replied.

Sid followed the coordinates that were overlaid on the image of the fossil site, and placed the drillscanners. Once he started them, they quickly sank into the ground as the laser cutters bit into the dirt and rock. A geyser of dust shot from the end as the drillscanners burrowed.

"Okay, done," Sid said. "What happens next with these things?"

"They'll scan the fossils underground and print out replicas with a 3-D printer," Hari said.

After a few hours spent digging for fossils in the VR lab, Sidney, Hari, and Penny were done with classes for the day.

"Did you see that rock I found with the feather in it?" Hari crowed.

"I still don't want to be a paleontologist," Sidney replied. "But I have to admit, that was pretty cool. There are millions of years of stuff trapped inside those rocks, and no one knows what it is until they uncover it. Drilling through the layers was like looking through a album of photographs—except the oldest pictures are at the back of the book instead of at the front. It's actually kind of like time travel."

"I guess that's one way to think about paleontology," Hari mused. "I never thought of it like that."

"It's hard to imagine all those creatures living millions of years ago, but if we could travel to the past, we could actually test our mass-extinction hypotheses and see what really killed them," Sidney said. "That'd be a pretty lethal field trip."

"Yeah, but the past isn't a place that exists somewhere," Penny said. "You can't just go to the past by walking through the right doorway. The things we use to measure time, like time zones, are human ideas that help us make sense of the world we live in."

As they walked back to the Tesla dorm for dinner, Sid continued to speculate. "So, Penny, you really don't think time travel is possible?"

"I won't say it's impossible," she said. "I'm just not sure how it could work. There's no road to travel along to get to the past or the future. We experience time because of the way our brains are wired. Time helps us order events that happen to us, so we don't go nuts trying to live our lives. The kind of time travel you're talking about only happens in books and movies."

"I'll just come out and say it," Hari chimed in. "I think real time travel is impossible."

"You guys have no imagination." Sid said. "I thought scientists were supposed to keep an open mind."

Penny grinned, "If it were possible, maybe you could go back in time and design a better nanobot. I'm going to destroy the one you're using now."

"I've seen your bot, Penny. We'll see who destroys who," Sid said, laughing a little more loudly than usual. He was actually pretty worried about going up against Penny.

"And then I get to face the winner," Hari said, his face looked eerily calm.

"How come we haven't seen your nanobot design, Hari?" Penny asked.

"You'll see it soon enough," Hari replied with a serene grin.

That night, Sid couldn't sleep. His mind was whirling at the idea of time travel. What if it *were* possible to travel through time—not just back in time, but forward! Seeing into the future? That would be lethal! No question.

He picked up the old-fashioned watch his mom had sent for his birthday. It had been his dad's, and Sidney often found himself watching the second hand run smoothly around the dial, marking time that would never be experienced again. Sidney had a vague memory of watching his dad take the watch apart and put the pieces back together. Now, the watch was the only trace of his father left after the fusion reactor accident that caused his disappearance. It had been a gift from his mom to his dad, on one of their anniversaries. The case was dented and scratched in the explosion. The leather strap had been ripped apart, requiring Sid to fabricate a new one on a 3D printer. Bits of dirt and leaves were ground into the watch, and there was a hairline crack in the domed crystal protecting the dial. There were even bits of leaf *inside* the watch, as if they had been pushed right through the titanium outer casing. But somehow, the watch was still keeping perfect time. His mom said she thought the force of the explosion must have ripped the watch from his father's arm, but Sidney thought there must be more to it. Aboard the undersea WAVElab, Sid's uncle Mitch had said that traveling across dimensions resulted in some kind of "residue" snapping back to the original dimension, like an elastic band stretched tight and then released. *Maybe the watch has some kind of residue from the explosion on it*, Sidney thought. He had run every kind of test he could think of on it. *Except for carbon dating.* There was something important about the watch's condition that was prodding his brain, but the answer danced just out of reach. But all this talk of the past had him wondering.

Sidney's brain refused to slow down and rest. He knew he had a better chance of sleeping if he just got up and did something for a little while to take his mind off all his crazy ideas. He pulled on some jeans, sneakers, and a sweatshirt, strapped on the watch, and walked outside the dorm into the cool night breeze coming in off the ocean.

Thinking back to his conversation with Hari and Penny, Sid felt his feelings about the past start to shift slightly. Maybe the reason he was so disinterested in the past was that his own past was so painful to look at. He held that thought at arm's length and wistfully studied it. He had been so young when he lost his dad, and he couldn't remember much about him anymore. His memories were blurry no matter how hard he tried to keep them clear and in focus. It was the everyday stuff with his dad he missed the most, and he knew his mom felt the same. *I just wish I could eat one awesome tuna-salad sandwich with him—and ask him every question in the world.* There had to be a way to understand what had happened to his dad.

Sidney looked up at the stars. There were thousands and thousands of them that he could see, and millions more he couldn't. He was still haunted by the glimpse he had caught of his dad in the alternate universe that had appeared while he was trapped on WAVElab. Sid had seen into a universe where his father was still alive and well, at home with Sid and his mom. For a few seconds, Sidney had thought of entering that universe, but he knew his real mom would be devastated. Showing up in the alterna-Sid's universe would have unhinged that family, and who knows what might have been different? It might be a universe where Sid's dad became an accountant instead of a scientist. Maybe Sid himself would be different, and that Sid might never take things apart or wonder about the universe.

Even though he knew it was the right decision, Sidney still felt a huge sense of loss that he hadn't before. It was one thing to barely remember his dad. It was another to have seen him alive and feel that loss again, fresh and raw.

Looking around, Sidney was startled to find himself in front of the fusion lab. With all the thoughts of his dad spinning around and around in his mind, he had wandered to the last place his dad had been seen. His father had been one of the Goddard Island scientists who had pioneered fusion power—until the reactor accident.

Sidney stared into the ID scanner as it verified the blood-vessel pattern in his eyes and confirmed his identity. After a moment, the outer door slid aside, rumbling softly. Sid walked to the huge windows of the observation gallery, and looked down into the chamber beyond. There it was: the nuclear reactor. Strange, the room was dark. *What's going on?* Sidney wondered. Usually, the reactor glowed with safety lights that warned of radiation and intense gravitational forces. Those lights were never turned off when the reactor was operating. A chill ran down his neck.

Something wasn't right.

Sid took the stairs down to the reactor level and walked through the inner door into a dark, cavernous space. The reactor sphere was suspended in the center of the room, about eight feet off the ground and tethered with steel cables. When the reactor was operational, the cables were detached, and magnetic fields kept the meter-wide sphere floating off the ground. It usually made Sid feel like he was standing inside an atom. Tonight, dim spotlights lit the area around the reactor, but the rest of the chamber was dark.

A hulking shadow stood close to the reactor. Sid held his breath. He waited for his eyes to adjust to the darkness. A familiar shape took form.

"Talos!" Sid called out to his favorite AI. "Hey, I think this is the first time I've seen you standing still for more than five seconds."

The robot didn't respond.

As Sid walked towards Talos, his concern grew. The AI's status lights were dark, and the ever-present soft glow from his eye shield was missing. The robot had been completely shut down. Talos never would have done that willingly.

Talos's right arm was frozen in position, as if he had been reaching for the reactor.

What are you doing, big guy? Sidney took a few steps around Talos before discovering the AI hadn't been reaching for the reactor itself. He had been trying to reach an object *on* the reactor. A small, black, rectangular box was affixed to the sphere. A set of numbers flashed on the side: 00:02:59. And then, after a moment: 00:02:58. Sid had a horrible realization. The box was a timer.

This does not look good.

Sidney heard a soft sound in the darkness. "Hey! Who's in here?" he called, his voice trembling slightly.

Someone was at the reactor control panel. Sidney reached to call Dr. Macron but realized he had left his voxpod in his room. He turned to run to the staging area, but the door closed before he could reach it.

He was trapped.

"What are you...what are you doing to the reactor?" he asked the figure in the darkness.

"Destroying it," a raspy voice replied.

"Why? Why would you do that?" Sidney asked, his eyes darting back and forth between Talos and the dark corner of the room where the voice was coming from. He heard the figure move towards him.

"Because this place is dangerous," the voice hissed. "None of you understand what you're meddling with. You think you can control the very fires of the universe with nothing more than the minds of humans? To capture and control the power of the atom, we must call on other universes, other realities, and other beings that have gathered the wisdom used to create the universe itself."

With a start, Sidney spied a small emblem tattooed on the figure's neck that glowed faintly in the dark chamber. It was the symbol of the Alchemists. He had to get out of there.

"The destruction of this fusion reactor will permanently turn the public against the research being conducted here," the figure continued. "The Alchemists will take control of handing out scientific advances and information to civilizations around the world. *We* will become the rightful holders of the torch of knowledge!"

"That's...that's crazy!" Sid said, fear entering his voice. "You could kill someone!"

"Change is always painful," the figure said. "If some are lost in the process, it will be worth it to bring the human race onto the path *we* are blazing to the future," the figure shouted.

Slowly, the figure backed away, disappearing into the darkness. Sid heard some metallic noises as the intruder escaped through the network of air ducts that ran along the ceiling. After a moment, Sid ran over to the ladder rungs attached to the wall of the reactor chamber and climbed up. When he reached the top, he saw the access door to the air duct had been welded shut. He couldn't get out that way. He quickly climbed back down and ran back over to the timer. It read 00:00:59.

I'm not going to make it out of here, Sid realized.

His mind went blank with terror. Destroying the fusion reactor might flood Goddard Island and the surrounding coastline with radiation, not to mention the damage it would cause if the reactor reached critical mass and detonated. Somehow, Sid had to get out and take Talos with him, but his feet felt as if they were glued to the floor.

Just then, the particle projectors came to life. They moved slightly as they automatically adjusted their focus on the reactor sphere. The cables holding the sphere rattled as the magnetic fields buoyed it. A glowing red circle appeared on the floor around the reactor, indicating the danger zone of radiation and magnetic forces. Sid saw with horror that Talos was standing just inside the circle. He knew the radiation and gravitational effects from the micro-black hole would severely damage Talos's neural web, disrupting the delicate pathways that were every bit as complex as those in a human brain. If he were exposed to too much radiation, Talos would be the robot version of dead.

I can't let that happen, Sid thought. Talos had brought him to Sci Hi, and Sidney had discovered that, in his own way, the AI had as much personality as any of Sid's human friends. Leaving him here would be like leaving Penny or Hari behind.

Without thinking, Sidney ran at Talos's unmoving bulk and jumped, ramming into the robot's upper body. Talos teetered for a second, finally tilting back like a giant redwood tree. He hit the ground with a metallic thud. Sid saw Talos's head had cleared the danger zone.

Just then, the reactor powered up to full. The particle projectors fired their streams of hydrogen atoms into the reactor sphere, where the black hole would speed them up, and they would collide, producing huge amounts of energy. Sid watched, horrified, as the reactor started to glow. There was no way he could escape from the chamber. He needed to find a way to survive, but he couldn't look away.

The device attached to the sphere detonated. The blast threw off the particle streams, destabilizing the reactor. Shafts of light shot out from the particle entry ports, and bolts of electricity arced from the sphere to the particle projectors. Sid could only see flickers of the reactor chamber as the strobe light illuminated the room.

Sid grabbed one of Talos's metal arms and tried to pull him. He could feel the tendons in his neck go taut as he attempted to move the robot toward the door, but Talos wouldn't budge. He was too heavy for Sid to move alone.

"Talos, wake up!" Sid screamed into the AI's face. "You've got to move!"

There had to be a way to move him, some kind of emergency procedure. Just then, he noticed a glowing exclamation point spinning in the air beside Talos's head. Sidney touched it, and glowing letters appeared: POWER FAILURE. RESTART? YES/NO. He jabbed the YES icon several times. "Come on, *COME ON!*" he shouted.

Suddenly, the robot creaked. Talos was trying to move! One of his legs straightened slightly. A dim blue glow emanated from the lens of his eye.

Sidney caught a glimpse of the timer. He had seven seconds left. A halo of energy had formed around the reactor, twisting and looping as if it were made of glowing string. The halo was getting larger, spreading out. One of Talos's arms reached hesitantly for Sid, grasping his shoulder. Talos pulled him to the floor and rolled over Sid to protect him. Sidney watched in horror as the seconds counted down and Talos powered off again.

The energy halo around the reactor blasted outward, like a miniature Big Bang.

Sid couldn't see anything clearly, but his stomach groaned as if it had been turned inside out. His skin felt like it was covered in ants. His hand looked like an inverted image, like the old photographic negatives. The shape of the chamber itself appeared to be stretched and squashed. Then, waves of dizziness washed over him before he fell unconscious and his head hit the floor.

36

CHAPTER 3

Sid swam groggily back to awareness. He blinked a few times, unable to see anything clearly. He tried to get up, but something blocked him. He looked around and saw Talos still frozen in place, with an arm protectively covering Sidney.

It all came back: Talos, the reactor, the mysterious intruder, the explosion of light.

Sidney crawled out from under Talos, stood up slowly, and looked around. There was a thick layer of fog drifting through the reactor chamber.

Keeping one hand on the wall for balance, Sidney walked slowly to the doors leading outside. He was still dizzy but feeling better. A stray thought ran through his mind: *Where's the guy that just tried to blast us to smithereens?* But he couldn't worry about that yet. He didn't know if anyone else had even survived the blast. Come to think of it, he wasn't sure how *he* had survived.

The main doors were shut tightly. Diffuse, dim light came through the glass. When Sidney pushed on the door, it hit something, as if there were another wall right behind it. He pushed again, harder this time, and heard a cracking sound. The door opened, and shards of ice fell to the ground. He stepped outside and gasped.

The entirety of Goddard Island was coated in a layer of ice. The island glittered like a jewel. The ice under his feet was hissing and bubbling into steam, and Sid could see the ice across the island was vaporizing rapidly. The sky above was a hazy blue. He blinked and squinted against the glare of the sun, which was cutting right into his retinas.

How can it be morning, he wondered, *when it was nighttime just a few minutes ago?*

He didn't see the familiar California coast. In fact, he couldn't see anything but water in every direction. The island appeared to have landed in a shallow lake or sea.

Usually, the water around the island was alive with gulls, pelicans, and other local birds. Porpoises, seals, and whales regularly swam around the island. But the air was heavy and still, and the water stank like nothing Sidney had ever smelled before. The oily water formed ripples that slowly crisscrossed the surface. Mats of algae floated in the distance, bobbing on top of the sluggish liquid. Sidney felt the beginnings of a headache beginning to throb whenever he turned his eyes.

"What *happened?*" Sid whispered.

Students and staff were starting to emerge from the various buildings and mill about on the school grounds, dazed looks on their faces. Sid ran down the steps to join the others as the mist cleared. Professors were gathering the students into groups, checking for injuries and confirming everyone was accounted for. Sidney quickly scanned the growing group of people filing out of the nearest buildings and spotted Dr. Petraglif.

"Hey!" He waved his arms as he ran toward her. "I need to see Dr. Macron right away—I saw what happened! Someone broke in and sabotaged the fusion reactor. Talos is hurt. You have to help him!"

Dr. Petraglif quickly sent a robotics team to monitor Talos and brought Sidney to find the headmistress of Sci Hi. Dr. Macron's office was filled with staff members having muted discussions in twos and threes. If Sidney hadn't been scared before, he was when he saw the world's best experimentalists and theorists looked as confused and frightened as he was. Image windows had sprouted like a forest, filling the room with bright graphics and numbers. The scientists wandered through them, brushing them aside as they discussed and discarded ideas. Dr. Macron looked up from a data stream when Sid and Dr. Petraglif entered.

"Sorry for the interruption, Dr. Macron, but I think Sidney may have witnessed whatever caused our current situation. You should hear him out."

Dr. Macron focused on Sid, her eyes locked and unmoving behind her glasses. "What did you see, Sidney?"

He told her about the fusion reaction, the intruder, and his threats. "Was anything recorded on video?"

"No," Dr. Macron said. "Unfortunately, the radiation and gravitational distortion destroyed all the data. Somehow, the entry and exit retina scans were also conveniently wiped."

"Can we ask Talos?" Sid urged. "He must have some record of what happened. He was right there."

Dr. Macron consulted her voxpod for an update. "Unfortunately, Talos is severely damaged," she said. "Not only is he suffering from radiation exposure, but there are definite signs of tampering. It looks as though he were somehow infected with some kind of recursive virus that just keeps circling and looping back on itself, totally controlling Talos's higher brain functions. That may have enabled someone to control him while his mind was basically trapped in a 'box' made by the virus. He's being moved into a repair bay while we assess the damage. He won't be telling us anything for some time...if ever."

"Are you saying he could...die?" Sid asked.

"It won't be the kind of death living organisms experience, but his brain may shut down and his personality would cease to exist. So, yes, *death* is probably as good a word as any to use." She sighed, "I'm sorry, Sidney, I know he was special to you." She patted his shoulder. "We'll do what we can for him. But right now, I need to figure out what has happened to Goddard Island and the rest of the world. Dr. Petraglif can take you back to the dorms. We're asking all the students to stay inside until we know what we're dealing with here."

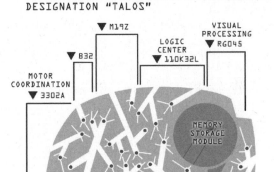

BRAINSCAN OF ARTIFICIAL INTELLIGENCE
DESIGNATION "TALOS"

▼ M19Z

VISUAL
PROCESSING
▼ RG045

LOGIC
CENTER
110K32L

▼ 832

MOTOR
COORDINATION
▼ 3302A

MEMORY
STORAGE
MODULE

THOUGHT
INTEGRATION

NEURON DAMAGE POINT

PROCESSING SPEED

Back in the dorms, Sid told Hari and Penny about his experience in the reactor chamber. The three friends compared notes about the inside-out feeling, the layer of ice that had evaporated in minutes, and the massive changes to the world around them. None of them were sure what it all meant or if it was even over. The world outside was eerily quiet. Nothing was flying, running, squirming, or crawling. The entire world looked dead. They had only been inside for a few hours, but they were already restless and eager to find some answers.

Penny asked, "Sid, that man you saw—do you think you could describe him?" She used her voxpod to open an electronic sketchpad in front of her. Her index fingernail lit up, ready to sketch.

"Yeah, good idea," Sid said excitedly. But his voice fell as he tried to recall what the intruder looked like. "Well, it was pretty dark, and I was scared out of my mind...."

"No worries," Penny said. "Just see what you can remember. Was his face long and thin, or round and chubby?"

"Long and thin," Sid answered. "His nose was kind of sharp." He sat beside Penny as she drew rapid lines that started to resemble a face. "Yeah. Yeah, that's good. Kind of chiseled-out cheekbones. I couldn't get a good look at his eyes because his brows were really heavy. Hey, I just remembered! He had a deep scar on the side of his face that went from the corner of his eye almost to his ear."

"Like this?" Penny sketched in more detail.

"Wow, Penny! That really looks like him! Creepy," Sid said. "You just need to add the glowing Alchemist tattoo on his neck."

"These guys aren't messing around," Penny said, sending the file of her sketch to Dr. Macron.

"We can't either. We need to figure out what happened to the Pacific Ocean," Hari said quietly. "Look outside. That water's only a foot or two deep, and it goes on for a long way. That's not our ocean. I don't even know if it's saltwater. Where *are* we?"

The three friends spent the rest of the day trading theories and discounting them just as quickly. Nothing made sense. And without being able to go outside and make any real observations, they were at a loss. They tried to pass the time, but the day went by painfully slowly.

Desperate, Hari finally asked, "Want to play catch?" after he spied a baseball and glove in the mess on Sidney's desk.

"Want to get in trouble?" Penny replied. "I'm pretty sure we'll break something if we throw the ball around in here."

"Not a good idea," Sid added. He loved baseball, but the baseball gloves and ball were like a slice from the parallel universe he had just glimpsed on WAVElab. They were a raw reminder of the alternate dimension where he had seen a version of his father throwing a baseball around. It was too private and painful to talk about it with Penny and Hari. He couldn't face sharing it and risk opening the door to the loss he knew was waiting behind it.

Reminders of his dad were everywhere—even on him. He was even wearing his dad's old watch. It made Sid feel close to his dad, but it was also a mystery he had been noodling over for years. Stuck inside Sci Hi, Sid's brain itch overpowered the personal attachment he felt to the watch.

Sid removed the watch from his arm and held it out to show Penny and Hari. "Hey, guys, you want to see something weird? This is the watch my dad was wearing when he disappeared. They found it in the wreckage. There're dirt and plant bits all over it, even inside it. There's even some kind of goo that got trapped under the little knob that winds it up."

Hari took it and looked at it up close in amusement. "Why would someone even need a gadget like this?"

"It's really old," Sid said. "From before voxpods or timechip implants, even."

"Hmph. Seems kind of silly to have a little machine that can do only one thing." Penny remarked.

"Well that's not really the point," Sid said. "The point is the accident happened in the fusion reactor, and you know how clean that place is. There wouldn't be any dust or debris that could contaminate the reactor mechanisms. But after the explosion, there were traces of dirt and leaves inside the reactor chamber, even inside the watch case, which was tightly sealed. How would it have gotten in there? The reactor chamber wasn't open to the outdoors. I'm sure those traces have been analyzed, but no one's ever said anything about it to me. I've actually been wanting to carbon-date it. Do you think we could try to check it out from here?"

Hari shrugged, "Why not? I'm starting to go really stir crazy cooped up like this."

"Me too," Penny said. "I'll bet we can get some time on the spectrometer in the Dyson building."

"Awesome," Sid said. He put the watch on his desk and used his voxpod to shoot magnified images of the watch through different filters.

Hari downloaded a mass spectrometer controller to their voxpods. "It's not going to be super-accurate, but it may tell us something."

Penny scraped off some of the substances on the watch and fed them into a slot on the side of her voxpod. "Right. Let's see what we can see."

They turned to the image wall. The spectrometer display came up, counting back the years as it homed in on the year the samples were from.

"Whoa," Sid said as the numbers rolled up the screen. "I don't understand this."

10,000…15,000…25,000…40,000…50,000 years ago… switching to new parent isotope…

"Where did your dad get this watch?" Hari asked.

"My mom gave it to him. It was her grandfather's," Sid said, "but I can tell you he definitely wasn't 50,000 years old."

The number continued to scroll.

350,000...450,000...550,000...one million years ago... ten million years ago...fifty million years ago...

"This is...this is...." Penny stammered.

"Crazy? Impossible? All of the above?" Sid finished.

The years flew past.

One hundred million years ago...one hundred fifty million years ago...two hundred million years ago.... The numbers slowed.

Samples originated approximately 230 million years ago. Samples identified as plant matter and insect blood. Accuracy +/- 10 million years.

"How is that possible?" Sid murmured.

Penny and Hari looked at him, their eyes wide.

Finally, after nearly eighteen hours trapped in the dorms, the intercom sounded "*Stand by for an important message from Dr. Macron.*" The large image wall in the room switched from an outdoor view to Dr. Macron's worried face.

"Attention, everyone. As you are all aware, we have experienced some sort of crisis we're still trying to understand. We are not yet sure what has happened to us, or the world around us, but we seem to have moved quite a distance from our previous location. We have lost all communications. Our equipment checks out, and at the moment we have no explanation for any of this. The ice coating the island appears to be some kind of byproduct of whatever effect sent us here.

The damage to the reactor formed an unstable black hole, which may have caused a wormhole to open. If this is the case, we do have some experience with navigating this type of incident. Right now, all that's clear is we're somewhere other than where we should be. Chemical analysis of the air and water seem to show a marked difference from what we're used to. The position of the stars is also different from where we expect them to be. We're not sure what is causing these differences, but we're working with several hypotheses. It's possible we may have experienced some level of...temporal displacement."

"Temporal *what*?" Sid asked. "What does *that* mean?"

"Shh," Penny hushed him.

"We have our top physicists working on this, but any and all ideas are welcome. Unfortunately, figuring out who did this will have to wait until we know what has happened. Our next task is to figure out a way to pinpoint our exact location... if we can...and reverse whatever process sent us here. If that's possible."

"Did she just say what I think she said?" Sid yelped. "Did we just travel through time?"

"What are you talking about?" Hari asked.

"Yeah, this is weird, but I didn't hear her say anything about time travel," Penny added.

"I'm pretty sure *temporal displacement* is just a fancy way to say time travel!" Sid sputtered. "Look outside! The ocean level has dropped almost to nothing. There's no animals anywhere. Look at the sky. There's some crud floating around in it, and it's giving me a headache. It smells weird, like something died and then burned. There aren't even any *bugs* outside! None! Do you know how impossible that would be?"

"So maybe some catastrophe killed all the living things," Hari said. "Maybe."

"Aren't you creeped out by this place?" Sid argued. "There isn't any sea life—at least none that I can see. Either everything in the world was wiped out in a few minutes, or we're someplace else. Could be the far past. Or maybe the future," Sid said. "Look, we've seen alternate dimensions! Why *not* travel through time?"

Penny wasn't having it. "Because there's no 'place' to travel to. The past isn't a location that you can get to with the right kind of vehicle. The only place the 'past' exists is up here," she said, tapping her head.

"You guys are no fun," Sidney muttered.

"You know what would be fun?" Hari countered. "Another round of Nanobot Death Match! It sounds like we could be here for a while."

"It's won't be the same without Talos," Sid sighed.

"We could all do with something to focus on until the boffins get back to us with what's really going on," Penny said.

"You're right, let's do it," Sid agreed.

"Brilliant! I'll tell the other floor monitors."

"Who's in the next match?" Sid asked.

"Me versus you," Penny said, rubbing her hands together.

Once the crowd had gathered, Sidney took a closer look at Penny's bot, called Medusa. It was taller than Sid's Crusher and had what looked like long, tangled "hair" very unlike Penny's own short, dark hair held in place with a headband.

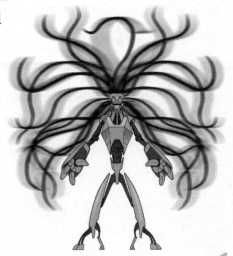

The match was a disaster—at least for Sidney. The Crusher's punishing piston punches were ineffective against Penny's Medusa. What Sid had taken for hair turned out to be whip-like electrified filaments that writhed and flailed about. The Crusher's control circuits were burned out, shocked into uselessness just seconds into the match. Sid tried to move The Crusher out of the way, but the nanobot wasn't able to respond. He was done.

Sid shook his head ruefully. Penny's nanobot had an effective attack feature. He hadn't thought about defense. "Good match," he said, shaking Penny's hand. "That is one tough bot. Takes after its creator, I guess."

He watched Penny's nanobot win three more matches, and then she was up against Hari's bot, Jack the Gripper. Hari's short, tubby bot had two massive arms ending in solid cylinders that turned out to be powerful electromagnets. Penny was joking and chatting as she adjusted her VR goggles, but Hari was completely silent, a focused look on his face.

Whoa, Sid thought. *I've never seen that expression on Hari's face before.*

Penny's Medusa started the match by attacking, filaments waving wildly about.

Hari tilted the Gripper's forearms toward Medusa, cranking up the magnets. Medusa was pulled off its feet, slamming into the Gripper's arms. Hari then reversed the magnets, repelling Medusa clear across the field and out of the arena for the win.

Penny sat there in shock with the goggles still halfway on her face.

Hari pounded the table with both fists. "YES!" he cried out. He held up his arms triumphantly.

"What just happened? Where's my nanobot?" Penny asked. "I didn't even see it. I want to see the replay."

The battle was replayed on an image window that opened above the table, and Penny watched her bot get tossed all the way across and out of the arena.

"*Nobody move!*" Penny used her voxpod to scan the floor and find the tiny machine before anyone stepped on it.

Penny joined Sid in the spectator's area to watch Hari's next bout, due to start in several minutes. "I didn't expect to be joining you so quickly," she said, disappointed. "I can't believe Hari was able to beat me in the first minute of the match."

"Can you believe that's Hari?" Sid said, amazed. "The Hari who never seems to get excited about *anything*?

"I've never seen him get so…intense," Penny said.

"So if there's another mass extinction, does this mean Hari and his nanobot might be the only ones that survive?" Sidney asked.

"It all comes down to the survival of the fittest," Penny replied with a sigh.

CHAPTER 4

The next day, the students were finally allowed outside their dorms, where they milled around looking at their strange surroundings beyond the perimeter of Sci Hi. The sky was filled with gray clouds, and off in the distance, lightning flashed. The lake that Goddard Island rested in was whipped up by gusting winds, splashing sudsy froth onto the rocky beach.

The oppressive, dingy sky filled Sid with foreboding, as if it were about to fall and smother him. The lightweight oxygen generators they carried with them helped to compensate for the higher carbon dioxide in the air as well as keep the worst of the airborne silt out of their lungs.

Around midday, Dr. Macron's voice emerged from speakers everywhere on the island. *"We've been working through the night to find where the wormhole has deposited us. Based on stellar positions and the chemical composition of the environment, we think we have a solid answer. Well, first, we have to rephrase the question. It's not 'where' we are so much as 'when' are we. By comparing star maps, the position and size of the moon, along with some other factors, we're pretty certain we have been thrown approximately 380 million years back in time, to the Devonian period."*

Sid shook his head, trying to make sense of it all. So time travel *was* real?

"The Alchemists have once again infiltrated our ranks and sabotaged our technology. But we will not let them hinder scientific progress. We're testing some promising hypotheses on how we might return to our own time. And the chance to explore prehistoric Earth with modern instruments is the chance of a lifetime...several hundred million lifetimes, actually. We're sending out a few aerial drones to do some recon, and if it's safe, we'll all be able to disembark and at least observe wherever it is that we've landed. As soon as we're sure it's safe to do so, we'll start letting groups go out to observe and document. Thank you."

"I guess one of us has to say it," Hari said, looking at Penny.

"Say what?" Sid asked.

"You were right," Hari replied. "Time travel *is* possible."

"I'll try not to rub it in," Sid said. "Honestly, I would have been happier if the answer *wasn't* time travel. Undoing this mess isn't going to be easy."

"I wonder if they've realized we're gone yet?" Penny asked quietly.

"Who?" Sid said.

"Our families," Penny said, looking at the floor.

"Well, geez, I suppose they must have by now, right? I mean, we've been gone for...well, how long *have* we been gone? How does that work?" Sid said.

Hari thought for a moment. "We went backward in time, so we would have appeared in our proper time right up to the moment we were thrown back in time to here. But the future hasn't happened yet. If we get back at the same instant that we left, we wouldn't appear to have left at all, except we'd have become a little older thanks to the time we've spent back here in the past. Does that make any sense?"

"Maybe," Penny said skeptically.

"Have you guys really thought about what this means? We're marooned almost 400 million years in the past," Sid said. "What if we can't get back? *Ever?*"

"I already miss my family," Penny said glumly. "I know they drive me mad, but everyone's family is like that."

Hari didn't say anything, but he wore a frown.

"What about you, Hari?" Sid nudged him.

Hari let out an exasperated sigh. "I doubt my family would even realize that I'm gone."

Penny was shocked. "You can't mean that!"

"I do mean it," Hari said. "Pradeep is the oldest son. He's in line to take over my father's firm. They've sunk everything into his future. I'm the invisible one."

"Oh, come on, Hari," Sid said. "If that were true, they would never have paid for you to come here, right?"

Hari snorted. "They're *not* paying for me to be here. I applied on my own and won a scholarship. My Uncle Rajeet gave me some money when he found out that I wanted to go here. He's my dad's little brother, and he went through the exact same thing. My parents don't really want me to be here. They're just too embarrassed to make an issue out of it because I worked hard for it, not because they handed it to me."

"Wow, Hari, I don't know what to say...." Sid began, but Hari waved him off.

"Forget it," he said. "I think the thing I'm feeling most right now is...*excited*. We're studying to become scientists, right? Sure, we're pretty much stuck here in the past, but we have the resources of this island. There are hundreds of people here with us; we're not alone. It's actually pretty amazing."

Just then, Dr Macron broke in again. "*Attention, everyone. After studying our situation and the event that moved us into the past, we believe we can reverse the process and return to our time. There isn't any guarantee our plan will work, but at* least we have a hypothesis we can test. It will take some time to prepare the reactor for a jump into the future, so we have decided to allow the students to venture down to ground level to explore this environment—cautiously. Our measurements show the air quality is tolerable, although it's not exactly what we're used to in our own time, so be careful as you acclimate to it. Report to your classes for specific assignments. That's all for now."

"Oh, man, this is *lethal!*" Sid said. "This is going to be like the most awesome camping trip EVER! C'mon, we have to check this place out."

"Let me just grab my voxpod," Penny said, "so I can do some sketching while we're out."

When they arrived, the teacher was so excited she was nearly jumping out of her skin. The three friends approached the teacher as an image window floated by her head.

"Ah. Gupta, Day, and Jamison," she chirped. "Let me see...." She consulted the floating window. "You're assigned to Quadrant 12B. That's just east of the dock, between the hydrogen tanks and the water purification plant."

"Dr. Petraglif, what is it we're supposed to be observing?" Sid asked. The mental itch of his curiosity was kicking in— big time. *Looking at old bones: not so exciting. Walking around in the actual 380-million-year-old world: lethally exciting.*

"Document any living organisms you see, using still images and video," Dr. Petraglif instructed. "You can also use the engineering department's new smell-capture technology to analyze the chemical composition of anything you find. There were several small extinction events in the Ordovician period, where we appear to be now. We know very little about the environment during this time, so look for signs of methane, bacteria, or volcanic activity that might signify a mass extinction is on the horizon.

"We don't know how long we'll be stuck in the past, and Goddard Island is going to start running low on food and water. These goggles will give you control of the sea and air recon drones we fabricated to identify water sources and organic matter we can use to replenish food and water supplies. We're sending out several students as scouts. You can stay here near the school, or even better, get out in the field and get some of that 380-million-year-old sunshine. It's a beautiful day out there! Be as thorough and as quick as you can. Dr. Macron told me this morning that we're going to try jumping back to our own time in about ten hours. Hurry, please!" she said with a wink that made Sid wonder if she would rather stay stuck in the past where she could study paleontology to her heart's content.

"Brilliant!" Penny cried.

"Don't need to tell me twice! Let's go!" Sid agreed.

Sidney, Penny, and Hari gathered up their equipment and headed for one of the huge freight elevators, riding from the buildings down the support legs to the giant floats that kept Goddard Island afloat in the ocean. In the shallow water, the floats were resting on the sand. With the tide out, the oily water was knee-deep around the island. The students could walk half a mile in any direction thanks to large sandbars that extended far out into the water.

During the trip down to ground level, Sidney studied the approaching shoreline. He looked around at the hazy, acrid air and the endless lake surrounding him. *This gross water is making that bacteria-ruin-the-planet theory sound more and more likely,* Sid thought. *At least in this time period.*

Outside, groups of large rocks were scattered around. The sand was pocked with stones and shells. The water was calm, and the gentle breeze carried the scent of the sea to them. No sign of methane gas yet. The students pulled on their boots. Puffy clouds provided occasional shade as they drifted in front of the bright sun.

"Ready to get your feet wet?" Sid asked with a grin. Hari and Penny groaned at his pun but eagerly sloshed through the shallow water to the nearest rocks to take took a closer look at the pools filled with tiny creatures.

"Look at this!" Penny cried, reaching into the water. She brought out a little creature with a lot of legs and a segmented shell. Two whiplike antennae waved from its shielded head while two large eyes, made of hundreds of lenses, stared expressionlessly. "I think it's a trilobite!"

Hari pointed his voxpod at the creature, and it said, "*This organism is* Calymene, *a trilobite.*"

"Lethal!" Sidney cried. They moved around the pool, observing a flurry of small aquatic creatures paddling through the water, and shooting footage of everything they found.

"Look at this!" Hari called, straining to lift a three-foot-long trilobite from the water. Its legs whirred, and its antennae twitched, slapping Hari's face. He dropped it back into the water, and it buried itself in sand.

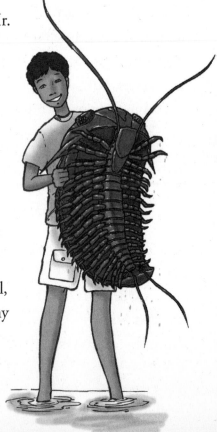

"That's a beaut, Mr. Gupta!" shouted Dr. Petraglif. "Don't let it escape without documenting it!"

"Hey, be careful!" Sid said. "We don't want to hurt anything here, just in case."

"Just in case what?" Hari asked, wiping trilobite slime off his hands.

"Look, this is time travel, right? Don't you ever read any

books? What if we do something back here in time and it affects things in our present?" Sid said.

"Hmm," Hari said. "I hadn't thought of that. That might be true. But what if time can flow around an event like a huge river that just flows around a rock? The river ends up in the same place it would have whether the rock was there or wasn't, doesn't it? Maybe time has the same flexibility, and minor changes don't alter the overall way things happen."

"I don't want to find out," Sid said warily. "Just watch where you step."

Penny busily sketched the creatures she saw, from the earliest coral reefs to mussel-like brachiopods. Small trilobites were crawling through the sand, tickling the tips of her boots. Their segmented exoskeletons had a metallic sheen that reflected a rainbow of colors in the sunlit water.

"Whoa, check this out!" Hari's excited voice grabbed Sid's attention. They watched a large millipede crawling over the rocks. Shiny black segments with bright blue markings were topped with a spiny pair of spikes. "That is one big arthropod!"

"Yeah, but there's not much else living here," said Penny.

"This is brackish water. No good for drinking," Hari replied. "I'm going to patch into a drone and keep looking for water inland."

"Okay," Sid said, climbing out of the water. "Tell you what: I'll try to find some food for us to take back to Sci Hi."

"Excellent thought!" Penny said. "Let's go. I actually want to see what else we can find out about this place."

Sidney, Hari, and Penny took their VR gear to where the submersibles were waiting to launch. They could be piloted by remote control, but they were also adapted for human pilots. The past had always seemed painfully boring. But now, up close to it, it was insanely interesting. Sid's curiosity was prodding him to find out more—up close. *What could it hurt to do a little hands-on research?* he thought. Sid ducked away from Penny and Hari as they were comparing discoveries with some of the other students and receiving control codes for the recon vehicles.

Sidney used his VR controls to open the hatch and jumped inside, dodging banks of equipment bolted to the sub's walls. The pilot's chair wasn't too comfortable, but Sid settled into it and brought the control menu up on his goggles. He was about to pilot a teardrop-shaped vehicle about ten feet long with fins at the rear. The front end of the little craft was dominated by a large glass dome housing cameras and all sorts of instruments for recording and measuring the surrounding ocean.

Glowing letters spelling out LAUNCH appeared to float in front of his face. He reached up and touched the letters, and his recon submersible slid into the water. Penny's sub splashed in right after his. She didn't seem to notice that Sid was no longer sitting next to her on the shore. He was actually in the sub—in the water, not on land.

Sid raised the goggles and look out through the dome. The water was a tropical-green color, with beams of sunlight reaching down below the surface. Swimming creatures too far away to identify glittered in the distance.

"*Hey, this is awesome!*" Sid said.

"*Brilliant,*" Penny agreed, her voice coming in over Sid's headset. "*Where are you, Hari? Are you in a sub or....*"

"*I'm flying!*" Hari cried. He was using his VR goggles to pilot an agile, wing-shaped aircraft from the ground. It was about the size of a falcon, and it was racing over the waves toward a barren-looking island. The drone had miniature jet engines that tilted when the operator wanted to hover and check out something interesting. Hari was enjoying the sensation of flying without actually being in the air and did a barrel roll just for the fun of it.

"*Whoever IDs the most creatures wins!*" Hari said.

"*You're on!*" Penny and Sid said simultaneously.

Sid was trying to wrap his head around the fact that he was exploring an ecosystem that had been gone for nearly 400 million years. As he headed down to the ocean floor, he turned on the powerful lights in the nose of the sub to reveal a colorful world. Outcroppings of coral grew attached

AERIAL DRONE

to rocks. Flat-armored fish wriggled clumsily in the sand. The little sub he piloted would scan each creature, identify it, and add it to the database that was being built at Sci Hi. In his headset, Sidney could hear Hari calling, *"Got one!"*

"Sid, look over to your right," Penny said excitedly. *"What do you think that is?"*

He ducked his head below a bank of switches until he saw what Penny had seen. *"Is that—is that some kind of squid? That's what it reminds me of, except for that shell, or horn, whatever that part is. It's almost like one of those whaddyacallits that we see in our oceans—you know, the squidlike things with the curly shell."*

"A chambered nautilus," Penny said. *"But this creature is* much *larger, and its shell is straight."*

"Yeah, it's huge. I wonder what it...." Sid pulled his goggles back over his eyes, and information about the creature appeared. *"Here we go. It's called* Orthoceras. *Man, it must be twenty feet long, and almost all of that is shell."*

A couple of large, silvery fish sped past. They were streamlined and dark gray with metallic, tiger-like stripes. Large, triangular fins just behind the gills looked almost like stubby wings. The fish tails were long and thin. They moved too quickly for Sidney to identify.

"Those are sharks! I can't believe it," Penny cried. *"They're being identified as* Cladoselache.*"*

"*Wow, there were sharks around this far back in time?*" Sid said. "*That's lethal.*"

"*Scientists think the decline of shark populations in our time could be a sign of a modern mass extinction.*" Penny noted, "*I want to take a closer look.*"

The long, conical shell of the tentacled orthocone twitched. Suddenly, it jetted away in the same direction as the sharks.

"*Hey, where's everyone going?*" Sid asked.

The display of the goggles showed a warning message. COLLISION ALERT was spelled out in red letters, with an arrow pointing to the left. Sid rotated the sub to see what was approaching, and the view tilted crazily as the sub was hit.

A huge fin passed by. Sid straightened the sub and peered into the blue water. A dark form became visible. It was a giant fish, the size of a fighter jet, with an armored head. As it closed in on him, Sid could see that instead of individual teeth, the monster's jaws were filled with slabs of bone that worked like the blades on a pair of shears. The sub identified the creature as *Dunkleosteus*, a 30-foot-long armor-headed predatory fish.

The fish swam off into the distance, disappearing in the murky distance. Sid's heart started to slow down a bit. "Wow, that was close," he chuckled.

Then, a dark smudge in the distance revealed the huge fish.

It was coming back. Fast.

"Oh, man!" Sid cried. He tried to steer the sub up toward the surface, back to Sci Hi. His heart was in his throat. There was no way he could outrun that thing. He spun the sub around and saw the fish's blade-like teeth opening wide.

Sid screamed as the fish slammed into him, shaking the sub like a tin can.

Red lights came on inside the sub's cockpit. Sid was in trouble. "*Hey, Penny, I could use your help here,*" he said, panic starting to rise in his throat.

"*Is that big fish going after your sub?*" she asked. "*Don't worry about it. The fabricators cranked out a lot of them. Just request a new one.*"

"*I can't,*" Sid said. "*I'm* in *this one. It was pretty great until this fish showed up.*"

"*What are you talking about?*" Penny demanded. Sid heard her removing her goggles. "*Where are you?*"

"*I'm in the sub!*" Sid cried. The fish was circling around again. "*I'm having trouble steering this thing. I think the rudders were damaged by the impact.*"

"*Have you lost your mind?*" Penny shouted. "*Hold on, here I come!*"

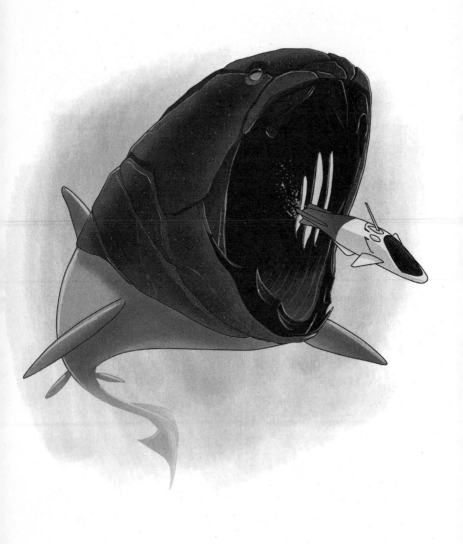

The fish was looming right in front of Sid, jaws open, when suddenly, bright lights flared right in its face. Penny's sub darted past him, ramming the giant fish. It turned and swam off again.

"*Whew, thanks*," Sid said.

"*Don't thank me. Get out of the water! Now!*" Penny shot back.

"*Right*!" Sid said. He turned the sub around and headed to Goddard Island.

"*Hurry*!" Penny cried. "*It's coming back!*"

Sid opened the sub's throttle all the way, and it leaped forward. He struggled against a pull to the left from the damaged rudder. He could see the temperature gauge showed the engine's heat rising, but he didn't dare slow down.

He looked at the rear-view camera display and saw the giant fish returning. Penny's sub was still distracting it, pushing it away.

Suddenly, the fish snapped at her sub, crunching down on the clear dome in front. The sub's lights went out.

"*Sid, I think...*," Penny started to say, but the fish had destroyed the sub's systems.

Sidney was getting closer to the docking arms on the island.

Just a few more seconds, he thought.

He could see the fish's armored head look his way, but he was suddenly jerked up into the air by the docking arms hauling his sub from the water.

That was a stupid idea, Sid said to himself.

"That was a *really* stupid idea, Sidney!" Penny hissed as he climbed out of the sub. "You could have been killed. What's wrong with you? You never think about consequences. You just plow on ahead."

"Sorry," Sid said contritely. "You're right, I was being an idiot. Heading out for real was too cool to turn down, though."

"Well, think next time," Penny said grudgingly. "I might not be around to pull you out of danger. Then where would you be? Fish food. Come on, let's get back to Hari."

Hari was still sitting in the shade, goggles on, flying his aerial drone.

"I just lost my sub to a huge fish," Sid said. Hari raised his eyebrows. "When we get back to our own time, if anyone finds a fossil of a minisub, that was me." Penny just shook her head.

"What is with you, Sid?" Hari groaned as he pulled off his VR goggles. "Your brain is like a factory that pumps out dangerous ideas. If you don't get it together, you're the one that's going to go extinct." Hari paused to listen to his headset. "Oops, looks like exploring is over. I just lost contact with the drone."

Suddenly, letters spelling out CONTACT TERMINATED flashed in their goggles. Dr. Petraglif's voice came through the tiny speakers in their heasets, *"All right, everyone,"* she said, *"that's it for the day. I'm returning all the drones to the warehouse. Dr. Macron has started the countdown until our next jump, which will occur in four hours. Students are needed to make sure Goddard Island is battened down and ready to jump."*

The three friends walked in the warm evening breeze to the warehouse that held the repair bays set up for the twelve Goddard Island AIs. One or two were standing in their alcoves, receiving software and neural upgrades. They nodded to the three friends.

Talos was lying on a sturdy table, with racks of machines surrounding him. Technicians bustled around, occasionally adjusting a sensor or a plasmoidal drip.

One of them said, "Just a few minutes. He's still undergoing deep neuronal reconstruction."

Digital readouts and gauges showed the various processes operating under Talos's outer metal skin. His head was open, and the delicate brain made of neural foam with millions of pathways running through it was visible.

Sid stood by Talos's shoulder, with his hands in his pockets. Penny and Hari looked at the various charts and readings. Everything pointed to the fact that Talos had been seriously damaged by the reactor explosion, the strange effects of the spacetime wormhole, and whatever the Alchemist had done to shut him down.

The AIs brain functions seemed to be operating at a very low level, just enough to keep his neural pathways active and functioning. There was an image window hanging over the giant robot that read 13 HOURS, 37 MINUTES, 19 SECONDS. That was how much time Talos's brain could exist at its current low-energy state.

If Talos's brain didn't improve quickly by utilizing its own diagnostic and repair abilities, it would suffer severe damage and would have to be decommissioned and replaced. A new brain would result in a whole new personality. The Talos that had brought Sid to Sci Hi and helped him acclimate to the school—the AI had helped him in countless ways and had most recently saved his life would be gone. Permanently.

I'm taking down the Alchemists if it's the last thing I do, Sid thought. *Someone has to stop them.*

"Talos. Can you hear me?" Sid asked quietly.

An image window appeared. Glowing letters formed:

YES.

"Do you know who damaged the reactor?"

YES.

"Who?" Sid whispered. "Who did it?"

I DID. I DID. IDIDIDIDIDIDIDIDIDID
IDIDIDIDIDIDIDIDIDIDIDIDIDIDIDIDIDIDID
IDIDIDIDIDIDIDIDIDIDIDIDIDIDIDID....

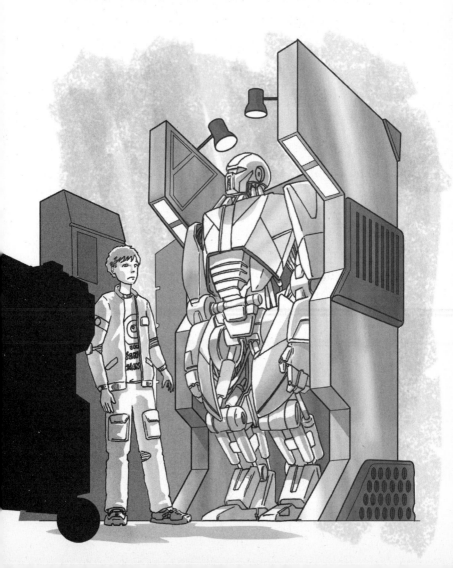

"No! No, that's not right! You were trying to remove the bomb, but you were shut down somehow." Sid said. "I was there, I saw you were trying to remove the thing!"

Talos continued to insist he was responsible.

"What did the Alchemists do to you?" Sid asked quietly.

"It's the recursive virus," the technician said as she walked up beside Sid. "His thought processes are caught in a loop. They just keep repeating. If we can't find a key to disable the virus, he'll never be himself again. The other AIs are all trying to crack the code. This could have happened to any of them."

The three friends exchanged a glance. They backed out of the room as the image window continued to print out Talos's feelings of guilt.

That night, everyone on Goddard Island congregated at the large main cafeteria to hear about the progress being made in Dr. Macron's efforts to return them to the present and to swap images of the weird creatures they had seen. A group of mathematicians, physicists, and cosmologists shared what they had concluded after hammering away at the problem of traveling through time. The equations and scribbled diagrams covered image windows across the dining hall. Together, they seemed to show that with the fusion reactor and the power they had available, there was no way to make the jump forward to their own time in one leap. The only way back would be to jump in stages, which would save up enough power and not destroy the repaired fusion reactor. The terrorist that had caused the damage had stranded them pretty successfully, and there were discussions about more possible plots to destroy Goddard Island. Whether they could actually make it back at all was still a question that was being chewed over.

The good news was that several scouts had successfully located water that could be chemically treated to create safe drinking water, and they reported a good number of large arthropods and fish that looked edible. The Sci Hi kitchen staff had set up a buffet with some of the foods the students had brought back and decorated it with a large myriapod shell from a huge, glossy black millipede that stretched almost five feet.

"Millipede-salad sandwiches," Sid said, picking up a plate. "This ought to be interesting."

Hari chose arthrodira fish tacos, and Penny selected a primitive plant salad.

They sat at a table near a window. Sid took a tiny bite of the sandwich and chewed gingerly. "Ugh," he said, spitting it out, "I can't bring myself to eat a bug sandwich."

Hari took a big bite of his arthrodire tacos. "Too bad. I was just going to challenge you to see who could finish theirs first. Actually, it's not too bad. It kind of tastes like chicken."

"I've been thinking," Sid said. "What if we got back to our own time *before* we'd been thrown back? There'd be two Goddard Islands, and two of all of us appearing in the same place at the same time. What would *that* be like?"

"I'm pretty sure it wouldn't be good," Hari said. "Who would be the 'real' you—the one born in that time or the one who landed there by mistake? And would the universe melt down if you came face-to-face with yourself?

"Here's one more thing to think about: How do we know for sure that we'd be returning to the same universe that we're from? It's not like there's a road map to guide us back, is there? We could end up in an alternate reality where the dinosaurs didn't go extinct and humans never evolved, or the black plague wiped out everyone instead of just a big chunk of humanity, or the sun is a tiny bit brighter and fries all life on the planet."

"How are we going to know?" Penny asked. How are we going to know—*for sure*—that we've made it back to our universe, not one that just *looks* like ours, but is still different in some way?"

"Stop, stop!" Sid cried. "My head hurts!"

Soon, it was time for them to attempt the first stage of the time jump. The three friends made their way to the

Tesla common area. The room was filled with students. Everyone was talking nervously. A huge image window showed a view of the reactor room, with scientists and technicians bustling around the reactor. Particle projectors arrayed around the room pointed at the reactor sphere. At the top of the image, a countdown was racing.

"Do you think this will work?" Sid asked.

"Not sure," Hari said. "The way the cosmologists kept interrupting the physicists, I don't think *they're* sure."

"How could they be?" Sid answered. "No one's actually done this before. I mean on purpose."

Sid sat on the floor beside the couch as the countdown reached zero.

"Right," Penny said tightly. "Here we go."

A diagram showed the particles first entering the reactor and then the tiny black hole at the center of the sphere. Suddenly, the black hole enlarged and then somehow deformed, changing its shape from a perfectly round sphere to a stretched and dented shape that blurred and wobbled. A blue string of light formed around the reactor, oscillating and jumping. The light string exploded outward.

Sid felt the hairs on the back of his arms and neck stand straight up. The inside-out feeling enveloped him again, but he recognized it this time and was ready for it. The dizziness grew, and he fell backward into blackness.

CHAPTER 5

Sid woke up feeling woozy, but okay. He staggered to his feet, wondering if the time jump had been successful. Were they home? The other students were still asleep or too groggy to start moving around. Sid shook Hari and Penny awake. "C'mon, you guys! Let's see what's out there."

"I feel like I was just hit by a truck," Hari grumbled.

"I feel like I was in the truck that hit you and then ran into a cement wall," Penny said.

Sid ran ahead and tried to open the doors, but the ice coating the island was in the way. Leaning in together, the three friends were able to force the doors open a little, cracking the ice, which fell to the steps. Sid squeezed out through the narrow opening, followed by Penny and Hari.

It was night outside. Gusts of wind drove falling rain into their faces. The dark sky overhead was thick with clouds. Bright bolts of lightning showed that Goddard Island had come to rest in a deep ocean. They could hear waves crashing into the island and taste the salt in the strong winds.

"What's that?" Penny shouted over the wild weather. She pointed toward the ocean.

"What's *what*?" Sid yelled. "I don't see—"

Multiple lightning bolts lanced down from the clouds, illuminating the water. Sid spotted some kind of creature breaching the ocean's surface—something whale size. The sound of its bulk crashing back into the water reached their ears, carried by the gusting winds.

The three friends looked at one another and simultaneously said, "Let's go back inside!"

By daybreak, the storm had passed, and the students were listening to Dr. Macron, who was on the image wall going through diagrams and maps that pinpointed their location. *"I know we were all hopeful, but I'm sorry to report that it looks like jumping into the future is going to be more difficult than we had expected. There seems to be some sort of effect that makes travel along the time stream into the future more difficult than going back in time, in the same way that rowing a boat against the current in a river is more difficult than rowing downstream. We're going to need more power than we had originally thought to jump forward to our own time. Before we go back to the drawing board, we'll check the atmosphere composition to make sure the air outside is safe enough. Once that's done, we may let you take some samples and images for analyzing."*

While he waited for the all-clear, Sid decided to drop by the Asimov building. He couldn't get the sight of Talos saying I DID IT over and over out of his head. He was worried about his metallic friend.

Talos was still standing in his repair bay. One of the readouts floating by his head showed his neural function was at 55 percent. Sid allowed himself to feel hopeful for a moment. Talos was definitely improving. *Maybe he'll be back to normal one day*, Sid thought.

"Talos, can you hear me?" Sid asked. Activity on some of the monitor readouts seemed to indicate that he could.

A grinding, staticky sound issued from Talos's speaker. Sidney was able to make out some words. "Th-this...is... T-Talos. Do you...ruh...require...anything?"

The AI turned his head slightly to see Sidney. He started to raise an arm, which pulled on several cables plugged into sockets in his forearm.

"No, no...nothing. Just rest, Talos," Sid insisted, patting the robot's arm. "I just wanted to see how you were...feeling."

"Thank you," Talos said, his faint voice crackling and sputtering.

Sid could see that Talos's brain function had smoothed out a bit. "You're going to be okay," Sid said quietly. He slipped away as Talos went back into standby mode.

As he left the Asimov building, his voxpod chimed. It was Penny.

"We just received the go-ahead from Dr. Petraglif. There's a hovercraft bringing some safari vehicles over to do some exploring. We've got seats on her truck. Meet us at the dock near Support Leg Three."

The ride to shore was a little choppy, but Sid could see that land wasn't far off. The sea smelled fresher, with whitecaps throwing spray into the air over the blue-green waves. Soon enough, the hovercraft reached the beach and lowered its landing ramp for the vehicles to drive ashore.

Within ten minutes, they were driving through rocky outcroppings and canyons formed from millions of years' worth of water erosion, and the cool breeze died down. The heat of the sun brought the temperature up quickly.

"When did Dr. Petraglif say we are again?" Sidney muttered, wiping sweat from his forehead. "The Perspiration period?"

"The Permian period, Sidney," the paleontologist chirped. "It is a bit on the warm side, isn't it? Earth's climate became much drier during the Permian, and there were large areas of desert."

Sid, Hari, and Penny, along with a few other students, were bouncing along the rugged terrain in a huge electric all-terrain vehicle that the Goddard Island 3-D printers had fabricated. It was high off the ground, riding on giant, thickly treaded tires. The truck had a sturdy roof, but the passenger and driver areas were open to the outside. Dr. Petraglif wrestled with the steering wheel, trying to keep the vehicle from overturning.

"The Earth had a varied climate during much of the Permian. We just happened to arrive during a time when temperatures were rising."

"Look at all the haze in the air, though," noted Penny. "It's like smog or something."

"That could be from the increased volcanic activity," Dr. Petraglif said.

Sid looked back the way they had come. Goddard Island rose above the ground on sturdy support legs, looking somewhat blurry in the haze. He yelped as Dr. Petraglif drove the vehicle down into a ravine. She shot him a wink over her shoulder.

"Doesn't she ever stop winking?" Sidney whispered. Penny elbowed him.

"Why haven't we seen more animals yet?" Hari asked. "I want to up my ID count."

"Most of the animals are likely spending the afternoon hours in whatever shade they can find," Dr. Petraglif said. "We'd see the same behavior from the animals in our modern-day deserts. There's one spot where animals might gather, even in this hot climate. I was so hoping we could study the adaptations of some of these creatures up close. Perhaps we'll see evidence of the traits that contributed to their extinction."

The big truck climbed up out of the ravine, and she stopped. "There," she said, shielding her eyes from the sun's glare. "That's a watering hole. If we can get close to it without scaring off the creatures, we might see what lives around here and maybe fill our water tanks so we can analyze it. The water will be filled with parasites and microbes. Lots to study, but there are probably a lot of things living in this prehistoric water that our bodies wouldn't be able to tolerate." She activated the truck's camouflage skin, making the huge truck virtually invisible to the creatures drinking and lounging at the watering hole. They edged closer slowly until they were just a few yards away from the creatures.

A variety of animals were drinking or lounging in the muddy water, moving as little as possible in the oppressive heat of the afternoon. Occasionally, a huge dragonfly would glide past them, diving low over the watering hole to pick off smaller insects. Sunlight reflected off their iridescent wings and shiny segmented bodies.

ALL TERRAIN VEHICLE

"Hey, guys, check this out," Sid said. "They all have two big tusks, one on each side of their mouths. It looks like they have a kind of beak, too. Are they all related or something?"

"They must be," said Penny, rapidly sketching the creatures.

"That's not true," Hari turned in his seat. "Think about sharks and dolphins. Their bodies are streamlined because they both live in the ocean, and that shape is suited for that environment, but they're not particularly related."

"Huh," Sid said. "Well, let's see what we can find out." He aimed his voxpod at the nearest creatures and compared them. "It looks like they could all be related. Umm...wow, they were...I mean they *are*...plant eaters. But those tusks look like they'd be pretty dangerous in a fight."

Penny nodded. "Sure, just like an elephant's tusks or a hippo's. There are plenty of animals in our own time that have tusks like that but are plant eaters."

"It looks like these creatures are from a group called *dicynodonts*," Hari said. "During the Permian period, they came in all different sizes, from rat size to bull size. The voxpod says they were really successful, up to the end of the Permian. But then almost all of them died out."

"What happened at the end of the Permian?" Sid asked.

"Mass extinction," Hari said. "A huge number of animals and plants were affected. Life on Earth was almost completely wiped out. Most of the species we're looking at right now are doomed, which is kind of creepy. One of the survivors will be *Lystrosaurus*. There's some lying in the mud over there." He pointed to some dog-size, tusked plant eaters taking a mud bath to protect their skin from the sun and biting bugs. "They don't look like much, but they must have been very adaptable to make it."

"What caused the extinction?" Penny asked.

"Good question," Dr. Petraglif answered. "Take a look around and tell me if you see anything that might cause difficulties for these organisms."

"Well, if there were enough particles in the air, wouldn't that block the sunlight?" Penny asked.

"Not enough sunlight would be deadly for plants," Hari said. "And then plant eaters would starve. And if *they* died out, meat eaters wouldn't be able to find food."

"Well, how do we know that enough plants were killed off for all that to happen?" Sid asked. "I mean, I guess it makes sense and all, but how do we *know*? I mean *for sure*?"

"Excellent point, Sidney." Dr. Petraglif said. "We think there may have been some bigger events, such as an asteroid, to have caused extinction on such a massive scale. But we can't be certain without more evidence."

All the creatures lolling around in the pond perked up, startled by a steady thumping Sid could feel inside the truck. A group of the strangest creatures he had seen so far waddled into view and headed straight for the water.

"What the heck are those things, and why are they *smiling* like that?" Sid asked.

The creatures were larger than a grown man. Their bulky bodies had short, stubby tails and were supported by four stocky limbs. A sturdy neck supported a thick-skulled head that had ridges and bumps. Their wide mouths were filled with peg-like teeth that stuck out, giving them what looked like a wide, toothy grin.

There were several large adults, and some smaller juveniles that happily splashed into the pond, disturbing the other creatures. The adults plopped down into the mud at the edge of the water, grunting and snorting.

Penny pointed her voxpod at the creatures. "They're called *dinocephalian*, but the exact species is unknown. Why would that be? The voxpods have been able to identify everything else we've seen so far."

"That's just been pure luck," Dr. Petraglif mused as she watched the animals enjoying the water. "The voxpods can only identify creatures that have had their fossils scanned and uploaded to the Goddard Island database, which is pretty extensive, but it wouldn't be realistic to expect that every species has been fossilized. Fossilization is actually a very rare process. Conditions have to be just right for it to happen. Earthquakes and volcanism destroyed many fossils. So really, it would be strange to *not* expect gaps in the fossil record. We will likely never know anything about most prehistoric creatures. That's why the recording and cataloging we're doing here is so important. This data is literally priceless!"

"Uh-oh...," Penny said, pointing to a rocky outcrop above the watering hole. A new creature was standing up, watching the various animals around the watering hole keenly. "I don't need the voxpod to tell me that's a predator. A *hungry* one."

"Whoa, that thing's huge," Sid said.

Hari was on it, pointing his voxpod to classify and record the creature. "I can't get a definite identification, but it's definitely a *gorgonopsid*. It says here that it's similar to... umm...something with a very long name...In...ino..."

"*Inostrancevia!*" squawked Dr. Petraglif. She took a quick look at the creature and started the truck's engine. "That's one of the most dangerous animals here in the Permian."

The creatures outside were spooked by the appearance of the fearsome reptilian predator. The bulky animals ran, scuttled, and waddled away from the deadly hunter, stampeding right toward the truck.

The predator raised its head and let out several hoarse barks before climbing down the bank to the pond. Several more of its pack appeared behind it. Sid could see threads of drool dripping from their huge tusk-like fangs.

The truck was stuck in some loose dirt. The wheels were spinning as Dr. Petraflif gunned the accelerator.

One of the huge, grinning plant eaters rammed into the truck as it attempted to escape, not seeing through the electronic camouflage coating that hid the vehicle from the creatures. Everyone aboard screamed as it tilted alarmingly onto two wheels. The camouflage circuits, damaged by the impact with the creature, gave out. The plant eater gave a surprised bellow and started around the truck.

One of the predators loped over and leaped onto the unlucky herbivore, slamming into the truck. Dr. Petraglif tried to raise the thick window shields. But it was too late.

Sid had a close-up view of the gorgonopsid, with its dog-like head. Upper and lower fangs snapped as it bit into the plant eater, spattering blood onto the windows. Penny leaned past him to snap several images with her voxpod. She was entranced and leaned out the vehicle window to touch the monster's skin. "Whoa!" she breathed as the voracious predator clamped down on the hapless herbivore.

"Hey, Penny!" Sid grabbed her arm and pulled her back inside the truck. He looked at her in amazement. He had never seen Penny so fascinated by something. Didn't she realize the creatures thrashing around outside might rip her arm off?

The truck rocked on its heavy-duty springs as the struggling creatures rammed into them again.

"Get us out of here!" Sid cried.

"Hang on, everyone!" cried Dr. Petraglif. She shifted down to the lowest gear and opened the throttle all the way. The truck lunged forward, spraying sand and pebbles everywhere. It climbed sluggishly out of the riverbed they had been driving in, almost tipping over as they reached the rim of the hill. The vehicle's transmission whined as it downshifted to get back to level ground.

The vicious gorgonopsids decided the truck was a juicier target than the plodding plant eater. They started loping toward the vehicle, trailing threads of drool.

The students screamed as one of the large predators leaped on to the vehicle's roof. Sid cried out as the creature's claws punched into the roof. The sound sent chills up his spine.

Dr. Petraglif swung the steering wheel back and forth, and Sid could hear the creature's claws sliding across the roof before it fell to the ground. It started to chase them, but soon gave up, snorting.

"Okay, we're good," Dr. Petraglif sighed and gave the students one of her classic winks.

"I've never been so scared in my life," Penny said, adjusting her glasses. "Or maybe it's excited. It's hard to tell!"

"What were you thinking, reaching out to touch that thing?" Hari demanded. You could have lost an arm."

"I'd just have to learn how to paint left-handed," Penny grinned.

"Well, if you lose a limb, don't come crying to me," Hari grumbled.

"Lighten up, Hari," Sid said. "She's okay, and we're okay. It was a tight spot, but we made it through."

"I'm counting those all as my IDs."

Sidney rolled his eyes.

When they arrived safely back at Goddard Island, the students had a short meeting with the biology and paleontology scientists, sharing what they had observed and recorded during their jaunt into the Permian wastelands.

Afterward, Hari asked, "When are we going to work on my nanobot? I have another match coming up tomorrow, and my bot needs some upgrading."

"Holy smokes, Hari, I think I created a monster with that tournament," Sid said. "I never knew you were such a competitive maniac. Okay, we'll work on it. Promise you won't kill me."

"After supper," Penny insisted. "I need to eat something and drink about a gallon of water. I've never been so thirsty in my life."

The next time jump was scheduled for early evening. The staff and students were determined to record and document the experience as fully as possible. The experience of jumping through time was still new, and the scientists wanted to collect all the data they could. In a flurry of activity before the jump, cameras, sensors, and recorders were set up at various points around Goddard Island. Some of the staff members took on an experiment and had hooked themselves up to record their brainwave patterns to track the effects of temporal displacement on the human brain as the jump took place.

The Sci Hi students were also keyed up, waiting for the next jump. They were enjoying their last taste of Permian air on the lawns. Sid, Penny, and Hari were out in front of the Tesla dorm with their friends, sitting on the grass as the sun sank down toward the horizon.

When a mournful siren wailed for a moment, marking the five-minute mark until the jump, everyone got up and went back inside. The three friends made their way back to the Tesla common room. Sid looked at Hari and Penny, who echoed his excitement and nervousness on their faces.

"Here we go," Penny said. "I actually can't wait to see where we go next!"

"Me, too," Hari said. "I'm hoping to spot some spiders in the next time period. I was so busy documenting all the other animals and plants that I forgot to look for my favorite arthropods!"

"I hope they aren't as big as that gorgonopsid!" Sid said.

"Jump in five seconds," said a voice coming through the image wall.

Tendrils of blue light began to cover the island, almost like wisps of glowing thread that floated downward and settled over everything, coating the buildings and trees in a cocoon of light.

Sid felt the weird inside-out feeling in his brain again as Goddard Island slid through a passageway in time. He was getting used to the sensation and was able to look around the common room at his friends. They appeared blurry and translucent to him.

Suddenly, the room rocked violently. They were knocked to the floor. Sid thought it felt like the air in the room was shaking somehow. The room shook and rumbled again, as if it were ramming into some immoveable object in the time stream.

Sid groaned as what felt like a metal file scraped through his brain.

One more violent jerk, and the room settled. A few small tremors passed through the structure.

Sid sat up, helping Penny and Hari to their feet.

"Wow, that was a dodgy trip, wasn't it?" Penny rubbed her head where she had banged into a chair leg.

"Where are we?" Hari asked.

"You mean *when are we*?" Penny replied.

"Why did it get so bumpy?"

"Let's go out and see," Sid replied.

"Tell me you're kidding," Hari said.

"I'm with Hari on this one," Penny said. "I don't think we should leave the building until we get an okay from Dr. Macron."

"*What?!* I can't believe you're the same Penny as the girl who couldn't *wait* to get a close-up look at a queen honeybee or risked losing her arm just a couple of millennia ago," Sid scoffed. "What happened to *that* Penny?" He turned to Hari. "C'mon, Hari...you're not going to let me go out there alone, are you? You're the responsible one out of the three of us!"

"No kidding," Hari said, exasperated. "That's why I'm saying that—*hey*!"

Sid was already squeezing out the door, grinning. "Hurry up, you guys—you know I'll probably do something stupid if you don't talk me out of it." He slipped out the door into the mist created from the time jump.

Penny shrugged and followed Sid. "We'll probably be all right. Probably."

Hari started after her. "That'll be perfect last words for the three of us," he mumbled.

CHAPTER 6

"Wow," Sidney breathed as he stepped out into the warm breeze. "I wonder when we are now."

Goddard Island had arrived in a huge fern forest, perched in the shallows of an enormous lake.

Tall, thick plants that reminded Sidney of bright-green bamboo shoots swayed in the breeze around the man-made island. Dr. Macron had given the students the go-ahead to explore, and they were wandering around the campus, taking in the unfamiliar plants and insects. The lake itself looked normal enough, but thick groves of horsetails grew out of the water near the shoreline.

Several small, squeaking shapes flapped by, chasing buzzing insects through the sunny afternoon sky.

"Are those...seagulls? Or some kind of supersize bat, maybe?" Sidney wondered. The little creatures moved so quickly that it was difficult to get more than a glimpse of them. They were white with turquoise feathers and black and red markings on their head.

Hari was able to scan one of the darting aerial acrobats with his voxpod. "They look like bats, but I don't think they are. What are those flying things called...umm... pterodactyls, or pterosaurs, right?"

"Look at the colors on their wings!" Penny exclaimed. "They're beautiful. Well, if we can find out when these things lived, we'll know where we are. I mean *when* we are."

"Let's see," Hari said. He opened his voxpod and scanned for the earliest pterosaurs. "They're flapping by so fast, it's tough to—okay, okay. Got it! These look like *Eudimorphodon* to me. If that's right, we're in the Triassic period."

A creature's mournful wail echoed in the breeze.

"What else lived on Earth at this point in time?" Penny asked, looking around warily.

Hari glanced at his voxpod. "Hmm, let's see. Amphibians, insects, all kinds of fish, some big reptiles, pterosaurs, of course, and Sidney's favorite Metoposaurus. Maybe we'll see the first Fluffy here!"

"Moving on!" Sidney scoffed. "What else does it say?"

"Whoa!" Hari continued. "This is when the first dinosaurs appeared."

"*Dinosaurs*!" Sid cried. "How lethal is *that*? We *have* to see one!"

"Don't get your hopes up," Penny warned. "I think Dr. Petraglif is going to be a bit more cautious after our run-in with that gorgonopsid back in the Permian."

The three friends made their way through the Sci Hi buildings, looking for the paleontology instructor. They finally tracked her down in the fabrication building, checking over the strangest vehicle Sidney had ever seen.

GYRO VEHICLE

It was a narrow, tall, segmented train with twin caterpillar treads positioned closely together on each segment. Each car after the engine was topped by five domes, where passengers could sit and look out at the environment.

"What do you think of our transport?" Dr. Petraglif grinned. "It's a gyro-balanced vehicle that should be able to navigate the dense forests we'll encounter. Dr. Macron has sent out a few recon drones and gave me the go-ahead to start taking out students. After our last experience with Permian wildlife, I've fabricated a vehicle that should keep us from becoming anything's lunch here in the Triassic. Once I've finished the vehicle checklist, we'll be heading out."

An hour later, Sid, Hari, and Penny were riding inside the gyro-balanced vehicle as it crawled through a tangle of trees, sunlight casting shadows on the transparent viewing domes. A double row of treads ran underneath each module, giving the whole vehicle the look of a huge caterpillar. The passengers sat inside clear domes that would provide protection from the creatures outside.

There was life everywhere Sid looked. Insects flew overhead, amphibians slithered through muddy ponds, and reptiles sunned themselves on warm rocks. He used his voxpod to record everything he saw.

Hari's voice came over the speakers in Sid's dome. *"A spider! I just saw a spider! The voxpod says it's an unknown species!"*

"*Excellent,*" Dr. Petraglif said. "*You'll get to name it, Hari!*"

"*I'll have to find out what 'Hari's awesome spider spotted during a time-travel accident' would be in Latin,*" Hari grinned, getting some video footage of the creature.

"*I'm a little surprised you didn't make a nanobot shaped like a spider since you like them so much,*" Sidney joked.

"*With eight arms of nanobot killing power, I would be unstoppable!*" Hari agreed. "*Good idea for next year's tournament!*"

"*Don't give him any ideas!*" Penny groaned. "*He's* already *unstoppable.*"

Sid saw something odd writhing through the ground ferns. "*Hey, Dr. Petraglif, can we stop for a second? I see something that looks like a snake, but it's floating about a foot off the ground. I can't see any kind of body attached to it.*"

The vehicle stopped, and the students were allowed to go outside.

Sid pointed out the strange creature to the paleontologist. "See? Look at that. It looks like a huge snake floating off the ground."

"Weird," Penny said. "I never heard of a snake like that."

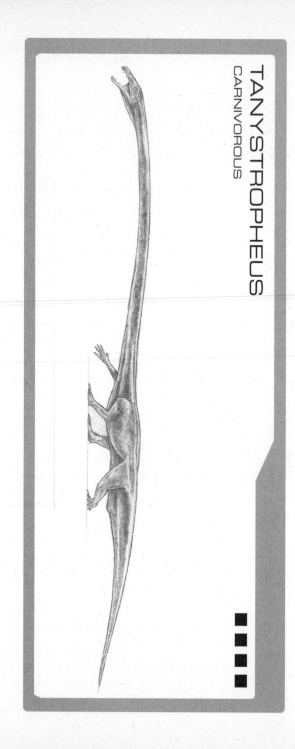

TANYSTROPHEUS
CARNIVOROUS

"That's actually not a snake," Dr. Petraglif said. "The body and limbs are hidden by foliage. It's a very odd reptile called *Tanystropheus*. That long head and neck is connected to a body with legs. It's probably heading for a pond or a lake. Tanystropheus may have been a fish eater. Just look at those teeth."

The creature's narrow snout was filled with needlelike interlocking teeth, perfect for trapping slippery fish.

The creature's body finally showed up, driven by short legs that moved the reptile slowly forward through the underbrush.

"I can't believe that thing can keep its head off the ground," Hari said. "How is it able to do that?"

The answer emerged when the reptile's tail emerged.

"It has an unusually thick tail. And with inflexible vertebrae in its neck, it stays balanced," Dr. Petraglif said. "Here's something to think about: Why do you think reptiles like Tanystropheus and the dinosaurs came along at this time? Why would they appear now and not earlier?"

"Well, I remember seeing something that I thought was kind of strange while we were in Mongolia," Penny said. "There were traces of fossil fungi in some of the rocks. I looked the fungus up in the Sci Hi database, and I found that fungus fed on dead trees. So that might be evidence of a massive number of trees dying off, right?"

"Sounds like a definite possibility," Hari said. "You may have just come up with a new theory to add to the canon, Penny."

"There are dead trees everywhere here," Sid said. "Could that be a leftover effect from an extinction?"

"It sure could," Dr. Petraglif said. "One of the interesting characteristics about Permian strata is that it contains large amounts of bacteria that fed on dead trees, at much higher levels than other time periods. Or perhaps there was too much methane in the air. It could be that whatever factors led to the mass extinction in the Permian involved conditions that killed off a substantial number of the world's trees. That mass extinction cleared away the earlier reptiles and opened the world up for new creatures to develop, like Tanystropheus."

Sid felt something hard in his boot. He sat down on a rock and took off his shoe, shaking the pebble out. As he pulled his shoe back on, he noticed something in the ground, something he didn't think was unusual at first. Then it hit him how impossible the thing he was looking at was. *Whoa*, he thought. The itch of curiosity exploded in his mind.

"Hey, Dr. Petraglif! Look at this!" he called.

"What is it Sid?" Penny asked, coming over to see.

"Nobody was over here before me, right? We were all looking at the Tanystropheus right over there. Take a look at this!"

It was a human shoe print in the cracked, dry ground, obviously left when the ground had been muddy and long before Sid and the Sci Hi group had arrived at this spot.

"Someone else is here," Hari said ominously. "Someone got here *before* us."

"How is that *possible*?" Sid breathed. "Could they still be around? We need to search for them!"

Dr. Petraglif used her voxpod to launch a search using the aerial drones flying ever-widening circles around Goddard Island's Triassic resting spot.

Sidney spotted several more footprints. "Check it out, guys! C'mon!" He raced into the dense forest. Penny and Hari followed.

"Wait, wait...!" Dr. Petraglif had to grab the next few students who would have plunged ahead. "We can't just go charging off into the woods here! It's too dangerous!" She sent a drone ahead to follow the voxpod signals of the three friends. "All right, everyone back into the vehicle, and we'll follow them," she commanded.

Sid kept running ahead, following the footprints. He burst into a clearing, where several dog-size creatures were feeding on something that had died. The predators were standing on two legs held underneath their bodies. Long, slender tails balanced the necks and heads held parallel to the ground. Two of the creatures studied them with big, bright eyes, cocking their heads at different angles to get a better look at the human intruders. One opened its mouth and chirped at them.

"Look at them," Penny said. "They're so cute!"

Sid looked at her doubtfully. "They don't look all that cute to me, unless by *cute* you mean 'bloodthirsty killer.' I wonder what they are?"

Hari pointed his voxpod at them. "Eoraptor, *an early dinosaur*," the voxpod announced. Its modern voicechip sounded strange and loud in the prehistoric jungle. Hari took a few steps into the clearing to get some video footage of the little dinosaurs. One of them lowered its head and hissed.

"Okay, okay. Relax, pal. We're not going to take your supper," Sid muttered.

Suddenly, the little predators all raised their heads in alarm, racing away from the clearing.

"What spooked them?" Penny asked.

"I don't know," Hari said, looking around. "I think we'd better get back to the vehicle."

"There's no time. Something's coming," Sid said uneasily. He could hear something crashing through the tree ferns and feel the vibration of footsteps on the ground. "We'd better hide. C'mon, get behind this fallen tree."

PRESTOSUCHUS
CARNIVOROUS
!HIGHLY DANGEROUS!

1357228.536
0061935
722647.6

107

The three friends ducked behind a rotted tree fern that lay at the edge of the clearing.

A huge creature broke through the underbrush into the clearing. Sid clenched his lips together to stifle a cry. The thing was gigantic, easily about the length of a city bus. Its body was held off the ground on four muscular limbs, the front two much shorter than the rear two. A thick tail swished behind it. Sid barely noticed anything beyond the creature's head, which was long and deep, with tiny red eyes placed high up on its head. The teeth in its top jaw were so long that they stuck out and curved over the lower jaw. The creature approached the carcass the Eoraptors had been feeding on, and picked it up, flipping it into the air and catching it in its heavy jaws. Sid could hear the bones crunch as the giant reptile bit down. It swallowed the whole thing in one gulp.

Hari slowly took his voxpod from his pocket and pointed it at the reptile.

"Wait, Hari! *Don't!*" Sid hissed.

"I just want to get one more ID." Hari replied.

"Let it go! It's just a game," Sid said. "We do not need to provoke that thing."

"I don't think this is such a good idea, Hari," Penny whispered.

"Prestosuchus. *Reptilian. Ancestor of crocodilians,*" the voxpod stated at full volume.

The creature's red eyes glittered as it cocked its head, looking for the source of the sound.

Sid, Penny, and Hari ducked under the fallen tree, hoping the reptile wouldn't spot them.

Sid was watching the creature closely, but something was tickling the top of his head. He reached up and touched something hard. He picked it off and looked at it. It was a shiny black millipede, almost a meter long, multiple legs wriggling.

Sid threw the arthropod from him, backing away from the tree, right into the clearing.

The *Prestosuchus* let out a warbling roar, and charged.

"Run!" Penny commanded, grabbing Hari's arm.

"This way!" Sid shouted.

Sid and Penny followed as he led them toward a huge expanse of fallen trees. They ducked under and clambered over the deadfall, skinning elbows, cracking shins, and bruising ribs. The creature loped after them, moving quickly despite its huge size. It crashed through the dead trees, splintering branches and smashing through rotted trunks. Sid tripped over a tree root and fell, narrowly missing a branch that would have skewered him.

"Get up, Sid! *Get up!*" yelled Hari.

Penny called out, "That thing wants to *eat* you!"

Sid could hear the snapping, cracking tree branches coming closer. The thuds of the ravenous reptile's footfalls shook the ground. He leaped up, glancing back for a second.

The creature was almost on him. He could see threads of saliva dripping from the thing's mouth as it charged. Its acrid breath gusted over him as it panted, and Sid nearly gagged at the smell of rotting meat. He leaped into motion, adrenaline jolting him to move faster and faster. He angled toward Penny and Hari.

A strange voice rang out, "This way! Over *here*!"

A man standing in front of a thorny tangle of fallen and broken trees was waving them over.

Penny and Hari ran over, watching as Sidney vaulted over a dead tree and reached them scant seconds in front of the Prestosuchus.

The man waved them into a small warren that was protected by a roof of sharp branches. Space was tight. Fallen trees hung overhead like a box of toothpicks dumped on the floor. The creature was too big to reach through the tangle of trees. It pawed furiously at them, circling around and over them, but it failed to budge anything other than a few branches. It emitted a rumbling growl in frustration.

The man held his finger to his lips. "*Shh.*"

Penny had to clap her hand over her mouth to keep from throwing up when a wet, sticky strand of drool dripped

onto her leg. The smell of the beast was overpowering, like a side of beef left to rot in the hot sun for a month.

After what seemed like forever, the creature snorted, as if to say "I wasn't really hungry anyway," and left in search of easier prey.

Sid breathed a sigh of relief at the creature's exit and the return of fresh air. He turned to study their rescuer more closely. The man was painfully thin, with wild hair and a shaggy beard. His clothes were torn almost to shreds. His shoes had holes in the sides. He was looking at the three friends like they were some weird kind of bugs.

"What—what are you doing here?" he asked.

"We saw your footprints and followed them," Sid replied.

"No, no. I don't mean right *here*. I mean here in the middle of the Triassic period," the man clarified.

"We thought *we* were the first people here, and then I saw your prints!" Sid's eyes narrowed in suspicion. "What are *you* doing here?" Sid's voice trembled slightly. If this guy was some kind of Alchemist terrorist, he could be majorly dangerous.

"We don't have time to get into that," the man said tensely, glancing around the dense forest. "It's vital that we get you away from here."

"Hold on," said Hari, holding his hands out to slow everyone down. "We're here by accident, but there are more of us, and we've got a safe zone. We can take you back to Sci Hi, and you can get some food."

"Whoa! Did you just say—Sci Hi? The Sci Hi that's located on Goddard Island?" the man asked slowly.

"That's right," Hari nodded. "You've heard of it?"

"More than heard of it," the man said excitedly. "That's where you're from?"

"Yes, we all are. I bet Dr. Macron would like to meet you," Penny replied. "You look like you could use something to eat. You'll be safe with us."

"Delphinia Macron is here with you? I can't believe this," the man said, covering his face with dirty, scarred hands. "You don't know how good it is to hear that name...."

"What, you expect us to believe that you *know* her?" Sid scoffed. *Who was this guy?* "So you've heard her name on the news. Big deal."

"I don't just know *of* her, I *know* her. I worked with her on Goddard Island, just when Sci Hi was getting underway. We were friends and colleagues."

"How long have you been here?" Penny asked. "What have you been living on?"

The man looked at the ground, thinking. "As near as I can figure, it's been seven or eight months. I lost track of the days just trying to stay alive. I've been living on bugs and fish, mainly, and whatever meat I can steal from the predators. I'm not that great at catching anything."

"How could you survive here by yourself?" Sid asked. "I can't believe that would be possible for long."

"I'm not by myself," the man said grimly. "There are two more people that are marooned here with me, although I wouldn't say they're actually *with* me. They're the reason I'm stuck here, and I need to warn Dr. Macron about them."

"We'd better get back," Penny said. "Everyone's probably worried about us by now."

The man stood up. "You're right. The sun's going to go down soon, and we don't want to get caught out here after dark. The bigger predators start to get active right around sundown."

They climbed out of their tree fortress and started walking. Hari took out his voxpod to locate the direction that would lead them back to Goddard Island.

"Wow," the man said, "is that a voicepod?"

"Voicepod?" Sid scoffed. "What's that?"

The man looked over Hari's voxpod. "This is a lot more streamlined and powerful than anything I ever used."

"*How* long have you been here?" Penny asked. "Voxpods have been around for years!"

"I'm not sure," the man said, doubtfully. "I'm pretty sure it's been less than a year." He shook his head. "I never thought I'd see people again. I mean, people that weren't trying to kill me."

"Trying to kill you?" Hari asked. "What do you mean?"

"I'll tell you when we're back with your group," the man said. "My name's Rob, by the way."

"Kind of like Robinson Crusoe," Penny said.

The man scratched his unkempt beard. "Yeah, I guess I am a castaway."

"Well, I'm Hari, this is Penny, and that's Sidney."

The man wiped his grimy hands on his tattered pants and shook hands with each of them.

"Huh," he said. "Sidney. I've always liked that name."

The animal noises coming from the trees and foliage were growing louder as the sun continued to set. Finally, they entered a clearing where they could see the spires of Sci Hi rising into the air.

The man stopped in his tracks. "Is that...is that...?"

"It's Sci Hi," Sid said. "The whole place got thrown back here, along with everyone on it. We're jumping our way back to the present, and this happened to be one of the stops along the way. Lucky for you."

Just then, Dr. Petraglif's gyro-track vehicle emerged from the trees. Her voice came from a loudspeaker on the vehicle. "Thank goodness we found you!" Then, taking in their new companion, she stopped, "Who are you? Students, return to the vehicle immediately!"

"Is...Dr. Macron here?" the man asked the paleontology instructor as she emerged from the vehicle cockpit, holding a shock prod.

"Not here in this vehicle, but nearby," she replied, looking at him strangely and glancing for a second at Sid.

The man turned to Sid, Penny, and Hari and said, "Look, I understand that you're all suspicious of me, but it would be much safer to continue this conversation indoors. I promise to answer any question you ask, but let's move."

Dr. Petraglif nodded slowly. "I can't argue with that. It's a prudent suggestion under the circumstances."

They boarded the truck, which began to snake its way through the Triassic forest back to Goddard Island. The mysterious intruder sat up front with Dr. Petraglif in the drive module.

During the ride back, Sid and his friends whispered about the mysterious castaway.

"Wow, can you imagine that?" Penny said. "Someone who got thrown back in time, like us! How do you think he got here? What could throw someone into the past besides a fusion reactor? I mean, is there anything else?"

"This isn't a time I'd want to be trapped in," Hari said. "Dangerous creatures, only eating bugs or lizards if you could even catch them, contaminated water. It's amazing he survived."

Penny glanced at him. "Don't you think it's weird he knows so much about Sci Hi? Maybe he worked there or was doing some research."

"Yeah, maybe," Sid mused. "But if he was thrown back in time, that means he must have been around when the first reactor exploded, right? I mean, he must have been working on the very first fusion project, and that was *ten years ago*! He said himself that he'd been stranded less than a year. I don't know. I don't trust the guy. He could be an Alchemist. This could be the guy that killed my dad!"

"Oh, come on…," Penny started.

"I hate to say it, but Sid could be right," Hari interrupted.

"I guess it's possible," Penny said. "We should find a list of the scientists that were at Goddard Island when the reactor exploded."

"Maybe we could find some clues in the evidence left behind after the accident," Hari said.

Sid stared into space for a moment, trying to figure out why Hari's comment had made his brain burn. Were there any clues from the accident? And then, it hit him.

"*The watch*! What about my dad's old watch?" Sid cried. "That crud stuck to it dated back more than 200 million years!" All the pieces began to fall into place. "My dad must have been wearing that watch when the accident happened! Maybe it got torn off when the reactor misfired and somehow got snapped back to our time."

Sidney stared at his friends, afraid to say the words forming in his head out loud.

"Are you saying that guy is your—" Hari started.

"There's a chance that man is my father," Sid finished, wonderingly. "I can't believe it." He gazed out at the Triassic landscape. A small flock of pterosaurs flew past, their leathery wings displaying flashes of white and orange.

"Wait," Penny said. "Some of this still doesn't add up. Your father disappeared ten years ago. Our mysterious castaway has only been here for eight months or something like that. And even if he is Sid's father, he might be from a different universe."

"That would mean he's even more lost than we are," Hari said. "He wouldn't have just been thrown back in time. He would be lost in another universe."

"It's him," Sid said, quietly but firmly. "I can't tell you why, but I know it's him. He's my dad."

CHAPTER 7

When they returned to Goddard Island, the mystery man was whisked away on a motorized cart to the Sci Hi infirmary. Sid, Hari, and Penny had to debrief, uploading all the images and video they had shot during the excursion. Sid was going out of his mind with impatience.

Unable to wait any longer, Sid ran to Dr. Macron's office, thoughts whirling. His father hadn't been killed by the reactor accident but thrown backward in time when the black hole in the reactor sphere had first been destabilized ten years ago, the same way that Goddard Island and everyone had just been thrown back into prehistory! So many questions were instantly answered, but Sidney felt a million more flying into his mind.

He burst into the office, ignoring the office assistant's call, "Hey, you can't just barge in...!" When he entered the huge, expansive room, he saw there was a group of people at one of the conference tables. The shaggy castaway was there, hugging Dr. Macron and talking a mile a minute.

"Delphinia, I can't believe it's you! It's been...well, I'm actually not too sure how long it's been," the man said.

Dr. Macron was talking at the same time, "You haven't changed! I can't get over it! It's like you've barely aged at all! I can't tell you how glad I am to see you! So much has happened, and I'm sure right now you'll want to see—" She gestured toward Sid as he entered the room, "Your son."

Sidney walked over slowly, stopping at the edge of the table and holding on for stability. No one said a word.

"Are you...are you *really* my dad?" he asked the man.

"I...I don't know," the man said, his eyes wide. "Delphinia—Dr. Macron, I mean—told me you were here. I can't believe it." He shook his head. "When I was stranded, you were so...*little*! You were *four years old*!" He stood up and came around the table. "Look at you—you're so tall. I missed all that time with you, Sid. I'm *so sorry*...."

Sid ran to him like a heat-seeking missile, almost knocking him down. "*Dad*! I can't believe it! I can't believe you're *here*," Sid cried hoarsely, over and over. He couldn't seem to hold onto him tightly enough. His voice broke into sobs.

Rob held onto him, overcome by his own emotions. "Is it okay if Sidney stays?"

"Of course," Dr. Macron said. "I think we should adjourn for a while."

Someone brought a chair for Sid, and he joined his dad at the table. Trays of food were brought in, and everyone gave them some space so they could talk.

"Is Mom okay?" Dr. Jamison asked.

"She's okay. She'll be so happy to see you again," Sid said, wiping his eyes. "She tries to hide it, but I know she still misses you. I wish I could tell her I found you!"

"We will," Dr. Jamison assured him. "I haven't felt this hopeful in months. Seeing you again is like solving the world's hardest equation. I never thought I'd do it, but I wasn't going to stop trying."

Sidney knew just what he meant.

He listened to his father's tale of how he had survived the Triassic period, and Sid explained how he had come to attend Sci Hi.

When he got to the part about how his mom had helped him get into Sci Hi, Dr. Macron broke in. "I want to see the Jamisons reunited as much as anyone. We all need to get back, and the way to do that is to get the reactor here powered up and ready to go."

Dr. Jamison nodded enthusiastically. "How can I help?"

"There's actually another development we should discuss first: Another group of students found two other people from our own time," Dr. Macron said.

"Where are they now?" Rob asked tensely.

"In our infirmary. They're being treated for dehydration, infections, and parasites. We'll need to do the same for you, once we're—"

"You've got to lock them up," Rob interrupted. "They're Alchemists. They're the ones that caused the accident that threw me back here in the first place. They hadn't planned on being caught in the blast themselves, but I showed up in the middle of their attempt to destroy the reactor. The explosive detonated prematurely. It caused some kind of rip in space-time and sent us all back here."

"They're not the only threat," Dr. Macron said worriedly. She mentioned the terrorist seen by Sid right before the reactor was damaged. "From what Sidney has told us about what he saw, the same thing happened to you. We've repaired the reactor sphere, and we're re-creating the time-jump effect in order to get back to our present. We landed in the Triassic after encountering some kind of disturbance in space time that caused our latest jump forward to fall short. It was a pretty rough jump, and some repairs have to be made to the reactor. There seems to be some effect, some force, that makes jumping forward in time require more energy than jumping back to the past."

"Your jump to the Triassic brought you to back in time to just a few months after I was stranded here. That would explain why I've been gone a matter of months, but to you, it's been ten years. Interesting," Rob said. "It's possible, since past events have been solidified in space-time, that there is less...friction...traveling backward than going forward in time, where events have many possible outcomes. Part of that turbulence effect may have been caused by the massive extinction event at the end of the Permian era. I felt the same kind of time turbulence that you did, but because my reactor was still just a small model, it didn't have the power necessary to push through the space-time turbulence, and I rebounded to land here in the Triassic. There's evidence that the Permian extinction was caused at least in part by an asteroid. That may have somehow caused some kind of ripple in the fabric of space-time."

"A ripple effect? Yeah, we know what *that*'s like," Sid muttered.

"It might be necessary to try to make it back in one jump, to blast through the turbulence," Sid's father said.

Dr. Macron shook her head. "The computer models we've constructed indicate a higher probability of success if the jumps are strung together. A single jump might damage the reactor beyond our ability to repair it. There's too much risk in trying to make it in one jump."

"Well, Delphinia, we worked on the original fusion reactor together. I'm ready to help, although if I've really been gone for ten years of your time, I'm bound to be a little rusty. But it'll be great to work with you again." Sid's father said. "We have some catching up to do. I want to hear all about what you've done over the last ten years."

"Mostly gotten older," Dr. Macron said ruefully. "You're right, though. It will be great to work together again. But first, the reactor needs to be recharged. We'll assign you quarters so you can get some rest."

"He can stay with me and Hari!" Sid said. "I can get a sleeping bag from the fabricators."

Rob nodded. "That sounds great, Sid."

"I'll send a med tech over to your room in a few minutes to treat whatever critters might be living on or in you," Dr. Macron said, standing up and dismissing the scientists. "We'll get you up and working in a couple of days." She took Sid's father's hands in hers. "It's so good to see you again, Rob."

As Sid and his father left the briefing. Rob said, "I'm starving. Let's go to the cafeteria. I have this weird craving for a tuna-salad sandwich."

Sid looked at his dad and grinned. "That's gotta be genetic. The tuna salad here is positively *lethal*."

"If *lethal* means 'good,' then I'm ready for it," his dad laughed.

Hari and Penny met them there. They were stunned to learn their suspicions had been well-founded and that the man they had met hundreds of millions of years in the past was indeed Sid's lost father. During their meal, they sat in rapt silence as Rob told them about his time spent in the Triassic period, including all that he had learned about the animals and plants he had encountered there. He was also full of questions about Sid's mom and how she had been since his disappearance.

After several rounds of tuna-salad sandwiches, the conversation turned to Sid and his friends and their experiences at Sci Hi. When lunch was over, his father made his way to collect some clothes and supplies from Goddard Island's fabricators. Sid walked back to Tesla with Penny and Hari.

"You must be so happy, Sid," Penny said. "Seeing your dad like this must be a wonderful feeling."

"I don't know...," Sid said. "I mean, *yeah*, of course it is. It's just...."

"Just what?" Hari asked.

Sid shook his head. "It's hard to explain without feeling like I'm a rotten person. It's just that my dad is a complete stranger to me. He disappeared when I was just a little kid, and I could barely remember him. I thought he was dead. Then to see him, alive, after I had never thought that it would be possible is just so bizarro, you know what I mean?

"The other thing that keeps running through my mind is how close I came to staying in that alternate universe when we were on board WAVElab. If I had done that, then I would have caused all kinds of trouble in that universe, and my dad may have been found in this one, but I wouldn't have been here. My head hurts just thinking about it all."

"Don't be so hard on yourself," Penny said, patting his shoulder. "Give it time. This is pretty much the weirdest thing that's ever happened to you, and you're both bound to feel a little strange as you get used to each other again. You can't unearth a 500-million-year-old fossil in a day. This is going to take time, too."

"Yeah, Sid, Penny's right," Hari chimed in. "Don't force it. You've both been through some crazy stuff, and it's going to take some time to sort through all that." Hari grinned. "Maybe you need something to take your mind off it. I need help modifying my nanobot for the next match. You up for a little robotics work?"

"Yeah," Sid said. "Yeah, that sounds really good."

They walked across the campus as small pterosaurs swooped and circled overhead. Back at their room, Penny helped Hari move his desk out to the center so they could modify Hari's nanobot. Sid tried to clear away some of his clutter from the floor and off his bed so they would have room to work. He opened his closet door to fling in an armload of clothes, but his eyes came to rest on the baseball gloves and ball. He suddenly realized why he had felt a sense of sadness, even after finding his dad, something he used to dream about. His sadness came from all the experiences he missed out on when his dad was gone. There were big occasions like holidays, birthdays, and vacations, of course, but it was the everyday stuff like watching a movie together, working on projects, and just goofing around that would have been so great. All that time together was lost, and now his dad was a stranger to him. It was unfair, but he knew the relationship he might have had with his dad might not be what he had imagined.

"Sidney?" Hari asked. "Are you okay? You've been standing there for five minutes. We need to get to work if I'm going to have my bot ready for the match against the Sagan dorm. Penny came up with a great idea, but I'm not sure how we can put it to use."

"Yeah. Sorry, guys. I was just thinking about something. What's your idea, Penny?"

"I was thinking that since Hari's bot uses magnetism, maybe we could develop something that uses magnetism to really give the bot some firepower," she said. "What about something like a rail gun?"

"A rail gun," Sid mused. His brain shifted gears from the emotional roller-coaster he had been on to the practical area of his brain that loved an engineering challenge. "That might work really well if we could build one small enough,"

Sid said. "We could use one of the bot's arms to run a magnetic pulse and fire a tiny piece of metal. But we'd need a constant stream of metal to eat through the kind of armor the nanobots have been equipped with. We won't be allowed to drop a pile of metal somewhere in the arena for your bot to reload. It's got to be something that...." He stared into space for a moment as ideas and options buzzed around in his brain. "I think I have it," Sid said. "How do you guys feel about cannibalism?"

"What?!?" Hari and Penny cried.

Sid held his hands up. "I'm not talking about *real* cannibalism! I mean, maybe the nanobot could use some pieces of itself, or of its opponent, as raw materials for the rail gun's ammunition."

"I think we could pull it off," Penny said. "It's going to be freakish, but that's pretty much your thing, isn't it? Remember the eyeball parasites?" She shuddered.

"I love it," said Hari, his hands in tightly closed fists. "Unleashing a storm of metal particles would be devastating! Deadly to the tenth power! *Victory will be mine*! My brother Pradeep would never think of a strategy like that."

"Whoa, settle down there, Space Marine," Sid joked.

They went to work modifying the nanobot, programming the micro-fabricator to produce the new parts needed.

There was a knock at the door. "Yeah, come on in," Sid called absently, focused on his task.

"Hi, guys," Sid's father said. "What are you working on?"

Hari explained the modifications that they were making to his bot for the next match.

Sid studied his dad. He had showered and shaved. His face was gaunt, with hollows in his cheeks that made it plain he had struggled to find enough to eat. His skin was weathered from the Triassic weather. His hands were rough and calloused. He wore a pair of jeans and a pullover shirt that accentuated his malnourished condition. He looked different from the old hologram Sid had taped up over his desk, but when he smiled, Sid knew he was the same.

"That sounds pretty awesome," his dad said as he admired the nanobot. "If you don't mind, I'm going to stretch out on Sid's bunk. I'm pretty beat."

"No problem, Dr. Jamison," Penny said. "We'll relocate to the common room. C'mon, guys."

Sid was the last to leave the room. He turned and started to say goodnight, but his father was already fast asleep, snoring softly. Sid watched him for a moment, then turned out the light and closed the door softly. It was going to be weird to have his dad back. No way around that. But maybe it would be good, too.

Several hours later, Sid joined his father outside a conference room in one of Sci Hi's administrative buildings.

"Hi….umm, Dad," Sid said. "It feels weird to be able to say that."

"It sounds just right to me," his dad replied. "Except you sound so much older than the last time I heard you call me that."

"Dr. Macron said to meet here. There was some kind of a surprise she wanted to show me." Sid looked through the large window, currently polarized into one-way glass, in the conference room. "Hey, there she is, in there. What's going on? Who are those other two people? They look like they're in the same shape that you are. But worse."

"Those are the two freaks that got thrown back in time with me," Sid's father said grimly. "I'm pretty sure they're Alchemists, but I don't have any solid evidence. Dr. Macron can't just take my word for something like that. After all, the reactor accident and time jump may have affected my brain somehow. She's just being a good scientist and testing the hypothesis herself."

Muted heavy footfalls came up behind Sid.

"Hello, Sidney," said an electronic voice.

Sid turned in astonishment. "Talos! It's so good to see you!" he cried. "*You* must be the surprise Dr. Macron was talking about. Are you okay?"

"Yes, Sidney, thank you," Talos replied. "It was kind of you to visit me during my recovery phase. I appreciate your steadfast support. The recursive virus planted in my brain kept me from realizing that I was not at fault for the reactor damage. Fortunately, it has been eradicated. Currently, my brain function is at approximately 87 percent of optimal. My own on-board diagnostic software is sufficient to complete the final repairs. Upon receipt of my infotainment voice app, I will be available to officiate at the next nanobot battle."

"Lethal!" Sid said. "Talos, this is my dad. Dad...this is Talos."

"Nice to meet you, Talos. You were still under construction when I went on my little time trip."

"A pleasure, Dr. Jamison. Is Dr. Macron questioning the other two castaways?"

"She's trying to, without tipping them off that we believe they're Alchemists. It appears she hopes they might give away some clues about the reactor accident and possibly what the Alchemists' long-term aim is," Dr. Jamison said.

In the conference room, Dr. Macron sat across the glass conference table, facing Alistair Churchill and Laura Birch, the two people found by the other research vehicles. The two new scientists were starting to suspect their story about being victims of an unfortunate science project gone awry wasn't working. Through an intercom, Sid and his dad were listening to the interrogation.

"What's going on here, Dr. Macron? We've been cooped up in this room for several hours. You have no right to hold us like—like *prisoners*!" Alistair Churchill insisted in a deep, gravelly voice, shifting his bulky body in a padded chair. "I demand you release Ms. Birch and me immediately!"

"I agree," Laura Birch said. "This is preposterous. I don't understand why you're treating us like this. We were stranded back in time through some sort of—catastrophe!" She ran a hand nervously through her ragged dark hair.

Dr. Macron said soothingly, "Nothing to worry about, I assure you. We needed to keep you under observation for a few hours to let the immune system amplifiers and parasite killer nanobots we injected into you take effect. Sometimes, people have allergic reactions."

"They're probably not going to buy that for long," Sid's dad muttered.

"They will not need to." Talos replied. He was remotely scanning Burch and Churchill. "The sensors placed in the adjoining room will transmit their physical state and, by extrapolation, their truthfulness." The AI was monitoring medical devices placed discreetly in the next room. The monitors could read a human's physical state from a distance without being connected to electrodes.

"Talos, are you sure you're up to this?" Sid asked. "Don't push yourself too hard."

"Thank you for your concern, but I am in no danger. I will have enough information to determine if Birch and Churchill are relating an accurate account of their experiences within the next two minutes."

Dr. Macron placed her voxpod on the table. "I have your work records here just so I can familiarize myself with your situation. I don't think I had met either of you before. Your records show that you were both referred to Goddard Island by Alkahest Associates. What kind of work did you do for them?" Through the one-way glass, Sid could see Dr. Macron lean forward slightly, her eyes intently focused on the two suspects.

Churchill rumbled, "Alkahest Associates is a consulting agency made up of professionals who are deeply involved in scientific inquiry in many fields. My specialty is tailoring software packages to the specific needs of elite laboratories around the world. Ms. Birch has a background in practical chemistry applications."

"He is lying," Talos said flatly. "Alkahest Associates is an organization with ties to the Alchemists. The word *alkahest* refers to a fabled substance that dissolves all materials and a source of interest for ancient alchemists. I will notify Dr. Macron, although I suspect she is already aware of this."

Sidney saw a red light glowing on Dr. Macron's voxpod. She opened an image window and scanned the information that Talos had just beamed over.

"So, it looks like they are Alchemists. I don't get it, Dad," Sidney said. "What is it the Alchemists want? What would make them so anti-science?"

"I've thought about that for a while. I think what it boils down to is actually pretty simple," his father said, watching the interrogation. "Science is all about explaining how things work, factually. The scientific method is a rigid framework. Everything's based on observations, experiments, and evidence. That's exactly what the Alchemists don't like. All they're interested in is controlling the rest of us. The most dangerous thing in the world to people like that is factual information that anyone, not just scientists, can verify. They don't want the rest of us to use our brains, because that makes people more difficult to lead."

In the next room, Churchill was getting upset. "We've told you everything we know. I demand you release us instead of wasting our valuable time with stupid, inane questions!"

They know something's not right, Sid thought.

The image wall between the rooms slid aside, revealing Dr. Jamison standing there. Seeing the one man who could identify them in the Triassic, the two Alchemists knew they had been cornered.

Talos strode smoothly over to the table, the shock absorbers in his legs softening the impact of his heavy metal frame. Churchill and Birch rose to their feet, nervously.

"Keep away from me!" Churchill spat at Talos. "What is the meaning of this?"

The intelligent machine grabbed the terrorist's arm and snapped on a flat black bracelet, with a tiny red light glowing on it. He did the same to Birch.

"These bracelets are for tracking purposes," Talos said. "You may access your living quarters and the food service areas only. All other areas of Goddard Island and the Sci Hi campus will be restricted. Attempting to enter any laboratory or building that has been deemed off limits will result in an electrical shock."

"Thank you, Talos," Dr. Macron said. The machine nodded to her and stepped back from the table. "We don't have the personnel to keep a watch on you every second, so this seemed like the most prudent course of action, unless you'd prefer being locked in a room until we return to our own time."

The two prisoners glared at Sid's father. "You think you've won, Jamison, but you're wrong!" Birch hissed. "You'll soon be crying for help from us. But alchemists only help those who believe."

"I don't know how you can believe in that Alchemist nonsense," Sid's dad said evenly.

"There's more at stake here than simple philosophy," Churchill said. "Although it seems you're all too blinded by your 'scientific method' to see it. How much do you think you'll be able to accomplish in your short, mortal lifespan? A few modest discoveries, maybe one significant breakthrough if you're fortunate. That's all. Sad, really.

"And what is it that keeps your knowledge seeking from moving past that point to true enlightenment? Time. *Time*. The human life span simply isn't long enough to put to use what it's taken a lifetime to master. At the very moment a scientist is at the peak of his or her profession, we are cut down. Our research is over. We never live long enough to make all the discoveries we need to."

Dr. Macro said drily, "So you walk away from science? How does that possibly further your cause?"

"Because," Birch said primly, "we need the reactor you've built and the staff of Goddard Island working toward *our* goals instead of the kind of folly currently being pursued here. The Alchemist organization consists of descendants of the first alchemists back in medieval times. One of their goals was to find something very important: the elixir of life."

"A fountain-of-youth potion? Really?" laughed Sid's dad. "You claim scientists are wasting their time doing genuine research while you crazies are searching for immortality. Wow."

"Your sarcasm is misplaced," Churchill sneered. "Based on medieval texts, we believe the compound we are searching for cannot be synthesized—in *this* universe. We need a way to explore other universes to acquire elements that don't or can't exist here."

"You people are *insane*," Sid blurted.

Churchill regarded Sid with narrowed eyes, reminding Sid of some kind of crocodile. "I see that this...*child* has been fully brainwashed into believing in your version of reality," he said disdainfully.

Sid leaped to his feet. "Hey, you nuclear fruitcake! For your information, science is the *opposite* of brainwashing. If you don't have evidence, you've got nothing but guesswork. If you *do* have evidence, you can change the world! Science isn't something you believe in because you're told to. You look at the evidence and then decide! Medieval documents aren't the same as solid evidence, no matter who your ancestors were!"

"Sidney, don't waste your breath on these two," Dr. Macron said, rising from her seat. "Unfortunately, they are beyond the reach of common sense or critical thinking."

"I'll remember this conversation when you've been in your grave for a hundred years," Churchill said. "In the meantime, do whatever you want. Try locking us in a cell. We won't be stopped."

"As Talos said," Dr. Macron said calmly, "you will be assigned quarters. You'll be able to venture outside and to the cafeteria. If you try to enter any other facility, you'll receive a little...negative reinforcement."

Birch looked as if she was about to be sick. Churchill's hands were shaking.

Hours later, Sid's head was still whirling with what the two misguided Alchemists had said. He turned to his father. "I still don't get what their problem with actual science is. I mean, *we did it*. We actually explored other dimensions, and the way we did it was with the reactor. *Scientists* build fusion reactors, not *mystics*. Why would they try to destroy the reactor if it could get them what they say they want?"

They were crossing one of the expanses of grass that connected many of the buildings on Goddard Island. Sid's father sat down in the shade of a palm tree, and Sid joined him.

"Sid, there are times when people will not make any sense to you. That's just how humans are. With these two particular people, I'm just not sure. I suspect that they wanted to damage the reactor so that it would need to be removed from its chamber and would be easier to steal from the island. After that, I'm not sure what they wanted to do. If you go back in history, alchemy was one of the fields of study that ultimately led to the scientific method. The problem is that aspects of alchemy are rooted in the supernatural, and the problem with the supernatural is that there is no physical evidence for its existence."

"So, it doesn't exist, right?" asked Sid.

"We just don't know," his dad said. "Science isn't the right tool to investigate any supernatural phenomenon, because science can only investigate things that are caused by natural events. The supernatural may or may not exist. From a scientist's viewpoint, it's better to say we don't know than to make a claim based on personal beliefs but no evidence. A good scientist always keeps an open mind."

Sid sat for a moment, digesting what his father had said. *I can't believe I'm talking about science—with my dad! How lethal is that?* His worry about how he and his dad would get along lifted a bit, and he relaxed. They had a lot in common, despite the lost time that existed between them.

After downloading a new voice, Talos was back as the announcer at the next Nanobot Death Match.

"In this corner, representing the Tesla dorm, in silver and black, the megamaster of magnetic mayhem:

JAAAAAAAACK THE GRIPPER, piloted by Hari Gupta! And in the opposite corner, that ambidextrous armored attacker with the awesome array of arms! Representing the Sagan dorm, in the blue and orange, piloted by Francisco Herrera...ARRRRRRRRRMED AND DANGEROUS!"

"C'mon, Hari, you can take him!" Sidney shouted. "Keep moving!"

Hari's bot was using the magnetic rail gun they had built into its right arm. The railgun sparked each time it fired. The molecule-size projectiles pushed the Gripper's opponent back against the faceted canyon wall, where it tried to raise a defensive shield.

The minuscule slivers of metal shredded the shield, then the nanobot itself. The spectators, viewing the match from one of the Tesla common rooms, were on their feet.

It was clear that Hari was going to win the match. His bot kept moving forward, slinging slugs into Francisco's bot until it was in pieces. Sid and Penny watched in amazement as the usually quiet and serene Hari once again gave way to fierce and aggressive Hari.

The match between the Darwin and Hawking dorms was being fought at the same time, and Hari would face off against the winner of that contest for the title of Nanobot Grand Master. He looked hungry for the challenge.

While the students were battling, the staff had been working hard. The reactor was fully charged and ready to muscle past the temporal turbulence at the border between the end of the Triassic period and the beginning of the Jurassic.

Sid's father was busy helping out with the reactor, becoming familiar with the more modern model and offering suggestions based on his prior experiences.

Sid lay in bed, trying to stay awake for the time jump, but he was asleep when the jump sequence was initiated. His dreams kept twisting into strange shapes like taffy that had been stretched and pulled and wrapped around itself. Nanobot versions of Birch and Churchill were flailing, trying to take down Talos. The third Alchemist circled them, passing in and out of the shadows. Sidney tried to warn Talos but his voice was lost in the warped spacetime. Suddenly, his dreams smoothed and became calm. In the real world, Goddard Island, tossed like a cork in a tsunami of space-time turbulence, broke free and appeared, coated with a cocoon of ice, in a tropical Jurassic afternoon.

CHAPTER 8

Sid's hair ruffled in the cool breeze as he skimmed over the wide river. He whooped as he increased the speed of his hydrofoil and lifted off the surface of the water, the fins on the elongated rudder acting like underwater wings. Penny and Hari pulled alongside him, laughing and shouting.

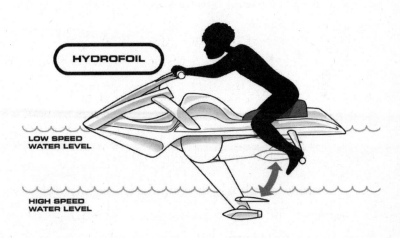

HYDROFOIL

LOW SPEED
WATER LEVEL

HIGH SPEED
WATER LEVEL

Upon their arrival in the Jurassic period, Dr. Petraglif had sent them out to look for possible signs of mass extinctions, but it was hard not to just have fun zipping around on the little vehicles the fabricators had turned out. The hydrofoils were about the size and basic shape of a bicycle without wheels. A telescoping tubular framework held the vertical stabilizer and horizontal fins that channeled the flow of water the way an airplane's wings do, causing the hydrofoil to rise up out of the water once it was traveling fast enough. Remembering his last adventure with the sub, Sid had vowed to stay above water this time.

The Jurassic afternoon was sunny and warm, but Sid could see towering thunderheads on the horizon. Occasional lightning flashes caused muted thunder that echoed from miles away. They would have to keep an eye on the weather.

The Jurassic period was packed with life. Huge pterosaurs glided overhead, occasionally swooping down to nab a fish just under the surface of the wide river. Creatures large and small lined the shoreline, drinking the clear water. Some of the animals sported armored plates, spikes, and other ornamentation that was brightly colored.

The three friends had brought the hydrofoils to the river flowing near the spot where Goddard Island had arrived from the last time jump. Sid could see some large creatures with plates along their backs drinking along the riverbank. Some had waded in and were cooling off.

Sid could see glittering schools of fish scattering beneath him as he climbed aboard the little vehicle and started its tiny electric engine.

"*This is* brilliant!" Penny's voice came through the radiobud in his ear. "*I can't believe what we're seeing!*"

The stegosaurs didn't seem frightened by the hum of the hydrofoils, but when Sid got a little too close to a baby stegosaur splashing in shallower water, it started squealing. A huge adult strode into the water, bellowing and swishing its spiked tail threateningly. It clearly thought Sid might pose a threat to its baby.

"Yikes," Sid yelped. He changed course, away from shore toward the middle of the river.

As he raced over deeper water, he saw the flashes on the water's surface weren't waves but something jumping out—something sleek and small.

"*They're squid!*" Hari said over the radio. "*They must be running away from something. They're all going in the same direction.*"

Sid sputtered as a slippery little squid slapped him in the face. "Yuck! I just got slimed," Sid laughed. More and more of the glittering cephalopods shot from the water, powered by their powerful jet-engine-like siphon.

Sid looked up as a huge shadow fell over his head, and he saw what looked like a gigantic porpoise sailing right over his head. "Whoa," he breathed. The enormous sea creature raised barely a ripple in the water's surface as its streamlined body slipped back into the water.

"I think they're ichthyosaurs!" Hari said. *"They look like fish or dolphins, but they're actually reptiles."*

Another of the huge fish-lizards broke the surface to Sid's left. He saw its huge eye fix on him for a split second before it snapped long, toothy jaws on a squid, splashing back into the water.

After a few minutes, the squid and ichthyosaurs veered off. Sidney's hydrofoil sliced through the water closer to the shore. He could see something huge emerging from the trees and splashing into the water, broken branches and green fronds torn loose from the trees.

A tiny, blunt head appeared several feet off the ground, held aloft by an extremely long, graceful neck. The tiny head and long neck were connected to a gigantic, bulky body supported by pillar-like legs that were churning through the water.

"Woo-hoo!" Sid crowed, turning his hydrofoil to dodge between the creature's legs the way he used to skimboard around trees in the snow back home.

Hari's worried voice came through his com, *"Sid, I don't think you should get too close to—"*

"You're telling me *not to get too close*?!" Sid replied.

"I learned my lesson! It's not worth the ID points!"

"Forget it, Hari," Penny answered him. *"He's not listening."*

"That's right, Hari," Sid laughed, *"I'm not listening!"*

He zoomed underneath the colossal beast, belatedly realizing that it was *much* bigger than he had thought. He could see its wrinkled skin, folded into deep creases. Pebbly scales formed a fine mosaic completely covering the creature. It looked like it was moving slowly because of its great size. As Sid passed beneath it, getting drenched by the splashes its legs churned up, he saw that it was covering a lot of ground with each step.

If one of those feet stomp on me, I'm going to be squashed like a bug, he thought.

He emerged from under the dinosaur in one piece but immediately encountered several more of the titanic reptiles, some huge, some smaller juveniles and babies. The littlest ones bleated in fear, looking behind them as they trotted as quickly as they could through the now muddy water.

Sid yelped as he leaned and shifted his weight to avoid ramming a young sauropod the size of an elephant. He swung around behind them with relief, but that relief turned into stark terror in a split second.

Three big, toothy meat eaters were striding after the sauropods, following them into the water. They were a dusty reddish-pink color with bold, black vertical stripes like some reptilian tiger. Blade-like crests poked up just in front of their eyes. Bright, dark eyes studied Sidney, heads twitching quickly like a bird's.

Sid screamed as the one closest to him lunged. Its powerful neck shot forward like a striking snake. He ducked under its snapping jaws, close enough to see every individual scale. Sticky threads of dinosaur drool fell across his head, causing a sudden lurch in his stomach.

Hari and Penny were shrieking something in his ears, but all he understood was *"...allosaurs...."*

It looked like the massive predators thought chasing this strange, swift prey was much more fun than the plodding sauropods. They followed Sid's hydrofoil as he turned and gunned the throttle, spraying up a sheet of salty river water. He dodged between the forest of titanic legs, hoping to lose the predators.

One of the allosaurs was knocked into the water by an adult sauropod's kick. It was quickly stomped on by the behemoth.

Sid could see Penny and Hari frantically waving to him from deeper water, safe beyond the herd of massive plant eaters crossing the river. He buzzed between the front legs

of a huge adult, and was almost crushed by a baby sauropod jostling to stay close to its mother. He glanced back in time to see a sauropod's tail crack like a whip across an allosaur's face. *Two down*, he thought. He steered out to deeper water, sure the allosaur would give up. He looked back to see the predator still behind him eyeing him hungrily, limbs dog paddling and strong tail swishing from side to side.

Oh, man, it can swim, he thought. Fortunately, his hydrofoil was faster.

The creature finally turned back at the middle of the river and paddled back to shore. By then, the sauropod herd was emerging from the far side of the river, climbing out onto the sandy bank.

"About time you stopped playing with your new friends," Penny said as he reached her and Hari. "We got a message from Dr. Petraglif. We have to get back."

The three friends started back to Goddard Island, hydrofoils lifting them clear of the water as they picked up speed. Sid could see other students racing back, rooster tails of water spraying behind their hydrofoils. After changing out of their wetsuits, Sid, Hari, Penny, and the other students streamed out of the docking area,

Sidney saw Churchill standing in the shade of a tree, silently watching the students troop by. Sidney stopped and studied him for a moment. His mental itch was on high alert, telling him to pay attention. *What is it he wants?* Sid thought. *Where is Dr. Birch?*

Churchill spotted Sid in the crowd of students. He smiled a slow, knowing smile, eyes half-lidded.

Sid felt a chill race down the back of his neck. Churchill creeped him out way more than the dinosaur that had tried to eat him. *He's planning something*, Sid thought uneasily.

Hari nudged him. "Come on. Let's go."

Sid hadn't had much of a chance to spend time with his dad once Dr. Jamison had been enlisted to plan the jump back to their present-day world, so Sid went to see how things were going with his work. He spotted his dad in some kind of meeting with other engineers and Dr. Macron in a corner of one of the warehouse-like buildings built around the reactor chamber. The scientists were gesticulating wildly, and Sid could hear raised voices. *Yikes*, he thought.

As he crossed the concrete floor, he heard a rustle of sound behind some crates. He spied some movement. When he checked behind the crates, whatever—or whoever—had made the sound was gone.

Sid's brain itch was still sounding off, sending chills down his back. He took out his voxpod and keyed in Talos's contact number.

"*This is Talos.*" The AIs voice said.

"Talos, this is Sid Jamison. Where are Churchill and Birch right now?"

"*Churchill is just entering the reactor building,*" Talos said. *He claimed to have information he needed to share with the reactor team, so Dr. Macron has allowed him limited access for the moment. Birch is in her quarters.*"

Weird, Sid thought. *If it wasn't either of them, who could it—?* Then an idea struck him: *Maybe the person responsible for sabotaging the reactor this time didn't escape and is still here on Goddard Island. I've got to let the others know!*

He drew a nervous breath. "Okay, thanks, Talos." He cut the connection.

When he reached the battling scientists, his dad saw him and waved him forward. Sid plopped down on an overstuffed couch to wait for the argument to simmer down a bit.

His father was in the middle of a heated conversation with Dr. Macron. "Delphinia, I absolutely hear what you're saying, but I'm telling you if you try to string this out over a series of time jumps, you're asking for a disaster! We risk damage to the reactor with *each jump.* And the reactor can't be repaired with the components we can fabricate ourselves, at least not here. We could be looking at being stranded in the past during a very dangerous point in the Earth's history! I think we need to jump back to our present in one jump—"

"Rob," Dr. Macron said, exasperated, "I understand, but there's no way we can collect, store, and transmit the necessary power to travel back all in one jump. Do you know what might happen if we try to make a jump like that and *don't* make it? We might become trapped in some kind of 'in-between' dimension with no way out! I think the safest course is to make a series of jumps, which won't stress the reactor and the power systems as much—"

Churchill's slow clap echoed through the cavernous space as he walked up to the group. "It is always a pleasure to watch you scientists flail about, caught in the quicksand of your so-called scientific method. You're blind to the other forces in—and out of—our universe."

One of the engineers seated on the couch with Sid remarked irritably, "So what was so important that you had to come here and interrupt our work? Or are you just here to stir up trouble?"

"Me? Stir up trouble?" Churchill's eyes widened innocently. "My specialty is software programming, not space time physics. No, I only meant to suggest that your scientific method might not be up to the task of to getting us back. You may need to call upon other...resources. Why limit yourself to traditional approaches in such a novel situation? I could, perhaps, be persuaded to assist, using some of the methods used by the Alchemists for a thousand years."

"Oh, come on!" the engineer rolled her eyes. "I'm not going to sit hear and listen to this—"

Sid's father held up a hand. "Churchill, I trust you about as far as I could throw you. Dr. Macron is giving you the chance to help, but she hasn't dealt with you like I have. If it were up to me, I'd have left you in the Triassic. But it's not up to me. So, go ahead, show us how pathetic our scientific methodology is. Show us the superiority of your Alchemist approach." He ran a hand through his hair, and stood toe to toe with the portly Alchemist.

Churchill looked around, sensing he had no chance to sway anyone to his way of thinking. "You're on your own, fools," he said coldly.

"Don't worry," Dr. Macron said mildly, "we'll still take you with us."

Churchill stomped off.

"He's up to something," Sid blurted. Everyone turned to look at him.

"Why do you say that, Sidney?" Dr. Macron asked.

Sid shook his head. "I don't know. Something about the way he looks at us all, it's like...he's planning something. We still don't know what happened to the Alchemist I saw in the reactor. And Birch just seems way too confident. I can't explain it. It just feels like they're not done trying to hurt us," he finished lamely.

"I know exactly how you feel," Dr. Macron said. "We can't waste any more resources on those two, though. We have our hands full trying to get home."

Several of the other scientists muttered their agreement.

"There is one thing we can do," Dr. Macron said. She opened her voxpod and brought up a com window. "Talos, this is Dr. Macron. From this moment on, I want you to personally monitor where Churchill and Birch are at every moment. I know they're wearing the shock bands, but I'd feel better if you handled this yourself."

Talos's voice replied, *"Of course, Dr. Macron."*

The meeting got back to the discussion at hand. After a few more comments, Dr. Macron said, "All right. I think that all of us are actually in a dangerous situation with Churchill and Birch and the unidentified terrorist who seems willing to blow up the island if he has the chance. We need to get back to our own time and turn them all over to the authorities before they make things worse for us. It was probably a mistake to allow Churchill and Birch the freedom of most of the island. Given those unknowns, I think it makes more sense to try to return to our present in one jump, as Dr. Jamison and several others think. However, I suggest fabricating several hundred high-capacity solar collectors and storage cells to augment our power supply should our power network be damaged by the attempt."

"I think that makes sense," Sid's father said.

After a few details were confirmed, the meeting broke up, and Sid left with his father.

As they walked across the Sci Hi campus in the late afternoon Jurassic sun, Sid asked, "Um...Dad, do you really think we're going to make it back home in one jump? Dr. Macron seemed pretty worried about it."

"She's right to be worried," Dr. Jamison answered, watching pterosaurs circle above Sci Hi. "It's a big risk either way. Making one jump requires a lot of power, but trying to string it out requires more power and puts more stress on the reactor, which is already weakened because of the sabotage damage. It isn't an easy decision. I'm going to have to go back in to help with getting the reactor system ready in a little bit, but I need to close my eyes for just a few minutes first. I'm beat."

As they walked back the Tesla dorm in silence, Sid was feeling downcast. He had only been reunited with his dad for a few days, but events were hurtling along so quickly and unrelentingly that he hadn't had many chances to just *talk* with him.

They got back to Sid's room. Hari was still out, working on his nanobot with Penny.

Sid rushed to pick up the stuff thrown all over the beds and floor. His father opened the closet door, and Sid tossed the stuff in. As he was closing the door, his father said, "Hey, what's this?" He held up Sid's baseball gloves and ball.

Sid was embarrassed. "Oh, that's just...that's, umm...."

"C'mon, it's still daylight. Let's try 'em out!" his father said.

"Really?" Sid said, surprised. "I thought you needed to rest."

"Are you kidding? A couple of minutes of catch is just what I need. Let's go."

For the next hour, Sid and his father tossed the ball back and forth, laughing and talking about nothing in particular. Sid saw his father perk up as they threw each other high flies, grounders, and line drives. He looked more energized, and the lines that had been furrowing his forehead relaxed.

As they walked back, they saw Penny, who was sketching a nearby pterosaur. The creature was devouring a fish it had caught on the grass near the reactor chamber.

"That's beautiful, Penny!" Sid's dad said. "You've really captured the color of that bill."

Penny looked glum as she regarded her drawing. "I don't like it. The wings don't look right, and I'm having a lot of trouble with the shape of its head."

"I think you're being too hard on yourself," Dr. Jamison said. "You've really captured the light and shadow, and the anatomy looks pretty accurate to me. Give yourself a break and just enjoy the process of drawing. If you enjoy drawing, you'll naturally get better over time."

Penny looked slightly mollified. "Well, thanks. I'll try to keep that in mind."

She joined Sid and his father on the walk back to the dorm.

Dr. Jamison left them at the door. "I'm going to get back to the reactor and help out with the jump. Thanks for the ball time." He turned and gave Sid a quick hug before walking off to the reactor building.

Sid stood, surprised at his dad's gesture.

Penny grinned, "Looks like you and your dad are starting to feel a little less like strangers."

"Yeah," Sid said. "Wow."

They went in and sat in the Tesla common room with the rest of the dorm's residents. They were all glued to the image wall that showed a camera view over Goddard Island. A clock in the corner of the image counted down the seconds until the jump.

Dr. Macron's voice came over the island-wide intercom. *"Attention, everyone. We're about to undertake our next, and hopefully last, jump toward our own time. In just a few seconds, we'll be on our way!"*

The counter reached zero.

"Here we go," Sid said.

The weird light show that came with the time jump flashed outside. Sid felt the strange inside-out warping of his thoughts, which was becoming familiar instead of frightening.

Then, something went wrong.

 **CHAPTER 9**

Sid groaned as he struggled to sit up. His head vibrated as if someone had placed electrodes on the sides of his head and shot an electric current through it. He blinked, waiting for his vision to clear. It was like looking at the world through a distorting glass of water.

"What happened?" Hari moaned.

"I don't know," Penny said. "The other jumps weren't like that."

Sid staggered to his feet. Everyone in the common room was sprawled on the floor. The image wall that had shown the outside view was just filled with static.

Sid's stomach rolled unpleasantly. "Oh, man. I'm gonna be sick." He stumbled to the nearest restroom, retching. After a few moments, the feeling passed, and he carefully walked back out to the common room, still feeling unsteady. The other students looked as bad as Sid felt.

Hari helped Sid break through the ice that had formed over the doors and the rest of the island. The first thing that struck Sidney was the heat. The time-turbulence ice was turning to steam as the sun struck it. Sid squinted into the hazy, yellow sky. Thick gray clouds occasionally blocked the sun. In the distance, Sid could see the sullen red cone of a volcano belching heavy black smoke into the air. Some kind of gritty dust blew in his face. He shielded his nose from the stinging particles.

Goddard Island was sitting on a vast, parched stretch of red dirt and rock. He could see animals moving around down on the ground, animals he had never seen in real life but countless time in museums. They were dinosaurs, big ones. A herd of duckbill dinosaurs was searching vainly for scraps of vegetation on the parched ground. A scrawny-looking meat-eater was hanging on at the edge of the herd, but it was too small to pose a serious threat, except maybe to the juveniles.

"This air is pretty disgusting," Hari said, rubbing red, watery eyes. "Look at all the junk blowing around."

Penny joined them, coughing. "This is horrible. Where are we, the end of the world?"

"As close as I think I want to get," Hari mused. "This must be the Cretaceous period. Those dinos were among the last to live on Earth before they got wiped out."

"So we're talking asteroid era? As in the really big one?" Sid said.

Hari nodded, "We probably don't want to stick around and confirm that hypothesis."

"What's all this crud in the air?" Sid complained, sneezing explosively. "It's disgusting. This can't be good. We were shooting to make it back to the present in one jump."

"Quite obviously, we haven't made it," Hari said.

"Let's go find my dad and see out what's going on."

"Good idea," Penny said.

A pterosaur passed above them. Not one of the gull-size ones from the Jurassic period—this monster was the size of a small airplane. It glided silently over the island and off toward some distant foothills.

The three friends set off for the reactor lab.

Inside, emergency lights cast a stark light on the reactor chamber. Scientists and engineers were running back and forth, exchanging panicked looks. A layer of thick mist hung just above the floor. Sid spotted his father at an image wall with some other scientists, looking over blueprints and schematics. As they approached, Sid could hear his dad's worried voice.

"…don't think it was time turbulence that stopped us. The *power supply* to the particle projectors was cut, and the

miniature singularity was deformed. That's what kicked us out of the time stream."

He turned to Sid, Hari, and Penny as they walked up. "Are you guys all right? That was a bumpy ride. We're obviously not back in the present."

"We saw some dinosaurs," Penny said. "Big ones."

"We're somewhere—or some*when*—in the Cretaceous period," Dr. Jamison said. "We're trying to pin down exactly when right now."

"Dr. Jamison, what happened? I thought we were going to make it back to the present in one jump," Penny said.

"It's like we hit some kind of brick wall in time," Sid said.

"That's pretty much what I think happened," his dad said. "Someone planted an explosive device to cut our power just as we hit the turbulence at the end of this time period. It stopped us cold. We can repair the reactor, but it's going to take some time. Don't worry."

"An explosive device?" Hari asked. "Do you mean some kind of bomb?"

Dr. Jamison nodded. "That's what it looks like."

"Why would someone try to keep us from getting back to our own time?" Sid asked.

"There could be a lot of reasons. For one, if we didn't make it back, all our fusion research would be invalidated. We'd look like we couldn't control the process when, in reality, all the problems surrounding the reactor have been the result of terrorism. The Alchemists wouldn't mind the destruction of Sci Hi, either. They would be able to step in and teach their 'pseudoscience' as if it were the real thing," Sid's father said.

"Have you talked to Churchill and Birch yet? I bet they had something to do with it," Sid said.

"We're rounding them up right now," Dr. Jamison said. "Birch has a background in chemistry that would come in handy if you needed to put together some kind of explosive. She's definitely a suspect."

As the three friends walked back to their dorm, Penny said glumly, "I wonder if we're ever going to get back. I don't know about you two, but I can't just go back to the dorm and wait until the reactor is ready again."

Sid glanced at her. "I know what would keep you occupied: a little exploring here in this time period. That will take your mind off the reactor, at least for a while."

"Are you loco?" Hari cried. "We were almost eaten back in the Triassic. What makes you think you wouldn't be killed here by some tyrannosaurs...tyrannosauruses...tyrannosauri?

You know what I mean! There are some crazy things running around here!"

Sid replied calmly, "Cool your jets. There's a way we can do a little reconnaissance mission without them being able to reach us. It'll take some time. I have to get something fabricated.

"I guess I wouldn't mind another chance at the nanobot championship," Hari said with a grin.

Penny sighed. "Sid, are you sure we won't get in trouble—or get eaten—or both?"

"Hey, come on! This is *me* we're talking about!" Sid protested, ignoring her rolled eyes. "I'll meet you guys back in the Darwin common room. They have the home court advantage for this match."

Sid ran over to the Engineering Fabrication and Design wing in the Dyson building. The EFD department took up most of one floor of the building, with the actual fabrication and manufacturing machines down in the basement. The place was almost empty, with everyone available either repairing the reactor and its subsystems or helping to transport the energy collectors in the path of the estimated impact shockwave. Sid found a workstation against the wall in the far corner of the department and sat down in a cushy swivel chair.

He logged in to the control system through his voxpod and scrolled though the huge list of available templates. When he located the one he was searching for, he opened it using the 3-D hologram projector on the desktop.

Fabrication templates were easy to modify. Sid looked at the specs for the gadget he was going to fabricate, selected small but powerful electric turbofan engines of the highest horsepower he could get, and then added superchargers and rocket boosters. He selected lightweight carbon fiber as the materials and paint with solar-collecting pigment. He then tweaked a few more options and sat back and looked over a hologram of the machine as it spun on the desktop. He frowned. *Something's missing*, he thought. He brought up one more menu titled "Exterior Finish" and selected neon blue, orange, and green for coloration, one color for each of the machines to be fabricated. *That oughta do it*, he thought. He hit the "Fabricate" icon and signed off the system.

A few minutes later, Sid sat poring over an image window from his voxpod. "Wow, this is going to be tough," Sid said glumly after seeing the Darwin team's bot.

"Hey, what kind of talk is that?" Hari said. "This is *me*, remember?" He was looking at the Darwin bot on the image wall. The thing was huge. It was named Evozilla for good reason. Sid looked at Penny and shook his head slightly. "That thing's almost big enough to see *without* an electron microscope."

"The bigger they are, the harder they fall, right?" Hari said. He was flexing his fingers in the VR gloves, his knuckles cracking.

"Just do your best, Hari," Penny said.

Talos introduced the combatants, his voice coming in over the Darwin common room speakers as he monitored several systems in the reactor sphere. "In this corner, in the green and yellow, the heavy-duty hurt machine: EVOOOOZILLLLLAAAA! And in the opposing corner, in black and silver, the terror of the Triassic! The junkyard dog of the Jurassic! The craziest bot from the Cretaceous— JAAAAAACK THE GRRRRIPPER!"

Evozilla was equipped with heavy armor, and with legs placed far apart, it had excellent stability. "Just don't let that bot get hold of you," Sid said.

The match started, and Hari immediately used the Gripper's rail gun. Tiny slivers of metal peppered Evozilla 's surface, pushing it back.

"Yeah!" Penny crowed, "Go get him, Hari!"

Suddenly, Hari was in trouble. Evozilla's thick arms telescoped out, and heavy claws closed on the Gripper, pulling it back in close. Evozilla's entire upper body opened, forming huge jaws lined with jagged metal teeth. The jaws bit down ferociously, chomping part of the roll bars from the Gripper's shoulders.

Hari fired the rail gun at the ground, which propelled his bot into the air, breaking Evozilla's hold.

"Your ammunition supply is down to about 60 percent," Penny said. "*Watch out!*"

Evozilla leaped like a flea and, in two bounds, reached Hari's bot. One of its telescoping arms shoved the Gripper back at tremendous speed, and it crashed into a faceted wall. Evozilla started to approach cautiously.

"I'm stuck!" Hari said. "One of the legs is caught," The bot's head tilted down, and everyone could see that one of the Gripper's legs had been impaled on a spear-like outcropping. Evozilla was getting closer.

The Gripper's rail gun sprayed the approaching bot with metal splinters. They were starting to eat through Evozilla's protective armor, but it was taking too much time. Evozilla kept coming, slowly, obviously hoping that Hari didn't have an inexhaustible supply of ammo for the rail gun.

The ammunition counter for the rail gun was counting down the shots fired, and it was getting close to zero. Evozilla kept coming.

"Guys, what do I do?" Hari said, worriedly. "I'm almost out of ammunition!"

The counter reached zero, and the rail gun stopped firing.

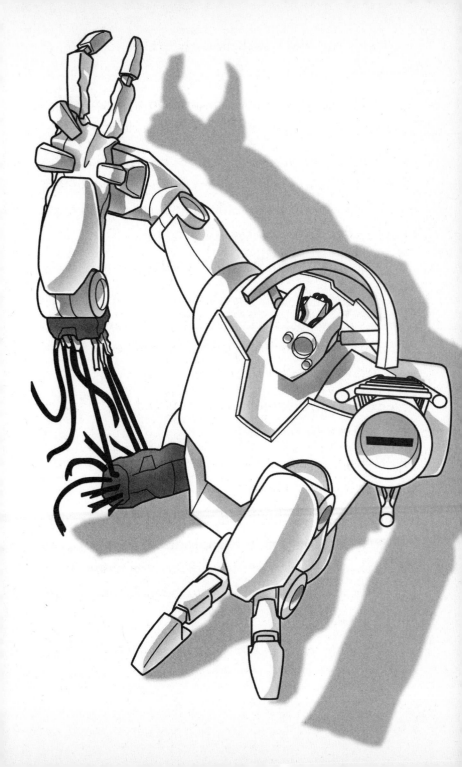

"Your leg," Sid said urgently. "Use your leg as ammunition stock!"

Hari reached the bot's arm down to the trapped leg, and ripped it free. The bot fell to the arena floor.

Evozilla shot out one of its arms. It stopped just short of Hari's bot. Hari fed the bot's severed leg into the chopper on its back. The chopper reduced the leg to tiny metal slivers, feeding them into the rail gun.

"The arms! Go for the arms!" cried Sid.

Hari brought up a targeting overlay, centering it on Evozilla's left shoulder. He fired, and the stream of metal shards sliced through the bot's shoulder joint before its pilot could react.

Evozilla 's right arm telescoped out and hit the faceted wall right next to Hari's bot.

Hari aimed and fired as Evozilla retracted its arm, reloading it for another try.

The metal particles from the rail gun cut through the Gripper's other arm just as it launched the arm again. Evozilla's arm tilted down toward the ground and fired. The rebound shot Evozilla high into the air, landing the bot outside the arena circle.

The Tesla students went wild, screaming and cheering victoriously.

Hari jumped to his feet, ripping off his VR goggles. "Yes, yes, YES!" he cried. He raised clenched fists in the air and screamed in delight.

Penny and Sid watched him, laughing.

"I think he's happy," Penny said.

"Really? How could you tell?" Sid joked.

They hoisted Hari up on their shoulders and walked him over to the Darwin team. They all congratulated each other, and Hari was presented with the nanobot championship trophy, which was too small to see without an electron microscope. A close-up projected on the common room's image wall showed a sparkling pyramid cut from a diamond chip with a microscopic cutting tool.

"This has been *so awesome!*" Sid cheered. "For the next tournament, we'll have to make the robots fight in shifting gravity fields, or maybe they can only use sound waves for weapons. Or how about we go the other way? We can make *giant* robots that the pilots ride inside!"

After the match broke up, Sid led Penny and Hari to the fabrication building. He found the objects he had commissioned wrapped in plastic, waiting on some pallets in a corner of the storage area.

He rubbed his hands together excitedly and pulled the plastic back. "Check it out, guys. This is what I was fabricating before Hari's last match. Jetpacks! What do you think?"

The jetpacks were blindingly bright colors, and looked like they were ready to leap into the sky all by themselves.

Penny giggled wildly with excitement. "*Brilliant*!" She was totally on board for the adventure.

"Of course, I customized the design template a little bit to get us maximum speed and maneuverability with minimum weight," Sid said. "This is going to be the closest you'll ever come to having a set of wings!"

Hari looked doubtful. "I don't know, Sid. Piloting an aerial drone by remote control is different from flying through the air *myself*."

JETPACK

"You can do it, Hari," Sid said smoothly. "The piloting system is really easy to use, and in an emergency, they'll automatically return to Goddard Island. What could go wrong?"

"I can't believe you said that," Hari said, rolling his eyes. "*A lot* could go wrong."

"I'll bet Pradeep never flew a jetpack to sightsee during the Cretaceous period," Penny wheedled.

A reluctant grin appeared on Hari's face. "I'm in."

"Lethal," Sid said.

They loaded the jetpacks onto a small electric cart and trundled out of the fabrication building.

"Just act casual," Sid said.

As they drove across the island to get to a secluded spot for takeoff, Sid noticed there seemed to be a lot of activity centered on the building housing the fusion reactor. Scientists were flowing out the front door, dispersing in every direction. Something about it made Sid uneasy.

"Stay here for a minute, guys," Sid said. "I want to find out what's going on."

He ran for the reactor building.

Inside, it was pandemonium. Scientists and engineers were frantically running with panicked looks on their faces. He found his father and Dr. Macron, along with a group of physicists, seated in a conference room. The were glued to an image window that showed three people in a small electric cart loaded up with boxes, driving away from Goddard Island. They kept looking over their shoulders as if they were worried about being followed.

"Hey, is that Churchill and Birch?" Sid blurted. "Who's that other—*hey*! That's the guy that blew out our reactor and hurt Talos!"

Dr. Macron said, "His name is Rudolph Keyes. He was one of the engineers working on Goddard Island. Talos was monitoring the bracelets, but he didn't realize they could be removed, since they were coded to him. We hadn't realized that the terrorist you saw had actually been transported back with us until now. Even though Churchill and Birch were monitored, this man Keyes was able to go where he liked without raising suspicion. Keyes evidently was able to fake Talos's ID, which he probably copied from Talos when he was tampering with him to deactivate the monitor bracelets. Talos didn't realize they had gone until he picked up on the stolen vehicle. Not only did he plant the explosive that sent us back in time, assault Talos, and free Churchill and Birch but he also removed a key control module from our reactor!"

"Well…can't you just make another module?" Sid asked. "Just…I don't know, fabricate a new one and fix the damage caused by the bomb."

"We have a bit of a time problem," Dr. Macron said.

"I'll say!" Sid exclaimed.

"I'm referring to a more immediate problem," she said with a smile. "We could fabricate replacements for the missing module and damaged components if we had sufficient time. The missing module would take almost forty-eight hours to fabricate because of its complexity. Powering up the reactor would take another ten hours. Unfortunately, we don't have the time."

"What's the rush? Don't we have like 65 million years to figure this out?" Sid asked.

Dr. Macron opened a new image window, showing the sky above Goddard Island. "See that light object there?"

Sid squinted at the faint crescent of an object just visible in the sky. "That's kind of a funny shape for the moon."

"It isn't the moon," Sid's father said grimly, zooming in on the faint object. "It's an asteroid. We believe it's the very asteroid that causes the extinction of the dinosaurs, and it's going to impact about one hour from now. If we can't recover the control module, repair the damage, and get the reactor powered up, we're going to have front-row seats for the collision. We're still making repairs to the reactor and power system. We don't have the time or anyone to spare to go after them."

A cold chill ran down Sid's back.

THE asteroid? If it was the asteroid they all thought it was, it wouldn't just confirm their hypothesis. It would cause an epic extinction that would devastate the planet. And the blast of energy released from the collision would kill them all before they had a chance to jump.

Energy release? Sid thought. "Is there any way to capture and use the energy released in the asteroid impact? If we timed it right—"

"*Yes!*" Dr. Jamison cried, jumping to his feet. "We had all those solar panels and power cells made after the last jump! If we set them out in the path of the blast, we could collect the energy we need and jump! It'll be more than we need."

"It would be very close timing," Dr. Macron said. "We'd have to factor in the time it would take to transmit the power to the reactor. It would have do be done in a split-second, but...maybe Talos could handle it," she said with a smile. "His computerized reflexes are exponentially quicker than ours. We can get students placing the solar collectors immediately. All that's left is getting the control module back. Birch and Churchill have a head start. We don't even have anything fast enough to catch them."

"Yeah, how could we—" Sid began, when it hit him. "Oh, *man*! I know how we can catch them!"

All eyes in the room turned toward him. "I had some jetpacks made so we could do a little exploring while we're here in the Cretaceous," he said, adding, "Well, I modified them a little bit. Hari and Penny are outside with them right now. They're totally ready to go!"

"No, absolutely not," Dr. Macron said. "It's much too dangerous for you to go out there, and there just isn't time. The asteroid is due to impact in fifty-eight minutes."

"That's exactly why I need to go! There's no time! We need that module, or we can't get home—you said it yourself!" Sid cried.

"*No!*" Sid's father shouted. "You are not going out there! I…I can't let anything happen to you…we just…" His voice broke.

"Dad, if I don't do this, none of us will survive!" Sid insisted.

"Then let me go," his dad argued.

"I made the jet packs for me and my friends. They're won't hold your weight."

"What about drones?" Rob suggested.

Dr. Macron looked at Sid's father, frowning. "I don't like it, Rob, but your son is right. Just sending the drones after them isn't going to be enough. They won't be able to take the module back if the Alchemists refuse to give it up. I think he can do it."

"There's no other way to get that module back in time," Sid insisted. "I want to get back to Mom, just like you do. *We can do this.*"

His dad shook his head slowly.

"All the evidence suggests this is the only way to make the jump," Sidney argued, sensing the decision was tipping in his favor.

"Evidence?" Dr. Jamison ran a hand through his hair and gave Sid a lopsided grin. "I guess I can't argue with that, can I?"

Sid smiled back. "Just thinking like a scientist."

"You got me there." Sid's dad gave him a crushing hug. "Be careful, Sid."

Sid hugged him back. "I will, Dad, I promise. I'll be right back."

Dr. Macron broke in. "Sid, I've sent the link to the drone that's tracking Churchill and Birch to your voxpod. No sightseeing—just find them, get the module back, and return as quickly as you can. I'll send along an aerial drone for protection. I think Talos would appreciate the opportunity to go after them. I believe his morphing abilities are fully intact now."

Sid, Penny, and Hari took their cart to the dock area of Goddard Island. Because this time, they had appeared inland away from any rivers, lakes, or oceans, the island was standing on its support legs about one hundred feet off the ground.

An aerial drone glided up to them, hovering patiently.

"Is that you, Talos?" Sid called.

The aerial drone tilted this way and that, waggling its wings in affirmation.

Sid put a combud in his ear, clipped a shock prod to his belt, and strapped on the lightweight jetpack. As soon as Hari and Penny had followed suit, Sid started up the jetpack's quiet, powerful electric motor. He turned the handgrip to open the throttle and floated up off the ground. "This is gonna be *lethal*!" he said, adrenaline shooting into his brain.

Penny lifted off like she'd been using jetpacks for years, a huge grin on her face.

Hari, visibly nervous, slowly lifted off. "*Have I ever told you two that I'm afraid of heights?*" he said over the com line.

"You'll be fine," Sid replied. "Just don't look down." He projected his voxpod in front of him as a translucent display that would help track down the terrorists. The timer read thirty-seven minutes until impact.

"It's payback time," he said grimly, stepping off the edge of the dock into open air.

184

 **CHAPTER 10**

"*Look at that!*" Penny called in Sid's voicecom. "*There's a whole herd of those horned dinosaurs coming up.*"

"Those things are huge," Sid replied. "They must be the size of gyro trucks."

They had seen a wild array of life in the few minutes they had been buzzing above the Cretaceous landscape, hunting for the Alchemists. Some, like the horned dinosaurs, were exotic, but some, like the bright-blue birds that flashed by, wouldn't have looked out of place in their own world.

"Look what's tracking them," Hari said, pointing off to their right. Hiding behind some dense, scrubby foliage, a group of tyrannosaurus watched the herd intently. There was one huge one and several smaller young adults and juveniles.

As they flew on, they passed a pack of bipedal dromaeosaurs in a clearing, their brightly colored feathers making them look almost like living jewels in the hot sun.

Sid and his friends were gaining on the fugitives. Soon, they were close enough to see a tattoo glowing on Keyes's neck. "That's him!" Sidney whispered to Hari and Penny. "That's the guy from the reactor! He's a whole other level of crazy."

"Right," Penny said. "How do you want to do this?"

"Send a message back to Dr. Macron and let her know we've caught up to them and that we'll bring the control module back shortly. Let's see if we can stop them in their tracks," he said turning to his voxpod. "Talos, will you do the honors?"

"*With pleasure, Sidney,*" Talos's voice relayed in his ears.

Sid lowered his altitude until he was just three feet off the ground and then pulled up behind the electric cart. Birch turned back and regarded him with surprise and shock.

"Wanna see some real alchemy? Watch us turn your cart into a useless hunk of metal!" Sid yelled.

Sid slowed his jetpack down to allow the aerial drone to close in to the vehicle.

There was a blinding flash of light as the drone fired its onboard laser drill at the cart's engine.

The vehicle jerked to a stop, sparks and smoke emerging from the engine compartment. It was done. Churchill and

Birch climbed out, rage on both their faces. He swooped in for a landing.

"Thirty-five minutes!" Penny called.

"This is what we're going to do," Sid said to the Alchemists through gritted teeth. "You're going to give me the control module you stole, and then we're all going back to Goddard Island so we can get out of here."

"I think not," Churchill said. "You're going to remain trapped here in the past, and the world's interest in Goddard Island's fusion reactor program will dwindle when they realize that it's too dangerous to implement. By then, everyone will know it caused two catastrophic accidents. We will have the ability to construct our own reactor based on your father's designs, and we'll be seen as the saviors of mankind when we make a gift of cheap, inexhaustible energy to the world. No one will question us from that moment on. They'll be too busy thanking us. I hope you're all comfortable here, because you're not going home."

Sidney's blood boiled at the thought of all his dad's hard work being used to make the Alchemists stronger.

"Listen," Hari said, "We're at *the* critical point in the Cretaceous period. An asteroid is headed directly toward us. All the evidence suggests this asteroid is about to wipe out about 80 percent of the life on the planet. We have to get back to our own time right now!"

Birch glanced up quickly and saw the asteroid, still a smudge in the sky, barely visible through the dust and floating ash particles in the sky. "I don't believe that for a second."

"No, this is the real thing," Penny insisted. "It's there, and it's coming in fast. We have to get that module back, and get *you* back. If you're here when that thing hits, you'll be as dead as the dinosaurs."

"You simpletons are so easily fooled by your scientific fairy tales," Churchill scoffed. "The Alchemists have documents tracing back thousands of years, and there has never been any mention of an asteroid impact at this point in time by any of the Alchemist clairvoyants or prophets. I just don't believe you. We have supplies that will last for quite some time, and we'll be very comfortable, I assure you."

"For people who claim to be interested in immortality, you're making a deadly mistake," Sidney said tightly.

"Run back to your cave of steel with the rest of your pitiful tribe of deluded fools," the third Alchemist, Keyes, hissed as he stepped away from the vehicle. He recognized the man's raspy voice from the reactor chamber just before they were all thrown back in time.

"I believe you've met Mr. Keyes," Churchill said smoothly. "As he says, you should go back. Your kind can't survive here. Your 'science' doesn't have much survival value in a place such as this."

"Fine," Sid said flatly. "Stay if you want. I just want the control module. If you won't give it to me, we'll zap you into a coma and take it from you. The raptors can fight over you after that."

Birch looked rattled, glancing uneasily toward Talos, who hovered above them in drone form. "W-what makes you th-think we haven't hidden the module somewhere?"

"Don't be dense," Penny said. "We've been tracking you since you left. We know you have it."

"I'm going to give you five seconds," Sid snarled, "And then Talos is going to shock you. One...two..."

"You wouldn't dare!" Churchill said, aghast.

"SHUT UP!" Sid shouted. "You'd better believe I'd dare. You ripped my family to shreds. Twice. For what? Because the work that my father and the others on Goddard Island didn't match up with whatever make-believe nonsense you freaks follow? I would love a little payback," Sid said. "That's three."

"I'd hand it over," Penny said.

"If you don't want to accept the factual information scientists discover, fine." Sid said. "You're free to believe your fairy tales if you'd rather. I draw the line at you attempting to kill the several hundred people on Goddard Island because they won't be led by the likes of you. I'll do whatever I can to show the world what frauds you are. That's four," Sid said, "Five. All right, Talos...Let 'em have it."

"Thirty minutes," Penny said tightly, looking at her voxpod.

The aerial drone slowly drifted toward the three Alchemists, silent as a dragonfly, its laser aimed squarely at Churchill.

"*Wait, wait!*" Churchill cried. "You miserable, misguided, meddling...*children*." He removed a padded envelope from his jacket and dropped it on the vehicle seat. Sid picked it up, removing the unit from the envelope. He held it up in the air so Talos could snap the unit up in one of its manipulator claws.

"I don't believe you would have zapped us," Keyes challenged. "You don't look like the sort that has the stomach for doing what needs to be done."

"Believe it," Sid said. "From now on, I am the Alchemists' worst enemy."

"Right," Penny said. "Twenty-eight minutes. Let's get out of here. We can't carry you with these jetpacks, but Sci Hi is close enough that you'll make it if you start now—I think."

"Yeah," Sid growled fiercely. "*Run.*"

"We're not going anywhere, and neither are you!" Churchill spat. "Get away from us!" He picked up a rock and threw it at Sid.

"The asteroid's going to hit in a few minutes, and all this will be gone!" Hari said. "Your only chance is to make it back to Sci Hi."

Sid glanced up quickly and saw the smudge in the sky had grown much larger.

Keyes took a step toward Sid, but stopped when the drone dropped protectively in front of the boy. He glanced up at the sky and, without a word, started running back toward safety.

Birch watched Keyes running, and looked over uncertainly at Churchill, who tried to grab her arm. She shook him off, and haltingly started to walk away toward Sci Hi. Her walk turned into a clumsy run. Sid could hear panic from her as she dodged fallen trees and boulders.

"*Fools*!" Churchill thundered in rage at the betrayal.

"Let's go," Sid said. "We don't have any more time to waste on these guys."

The three friends rose into the air and zipped back to the school, pushing the jetpacks to their limit. They flew over the rows of energy collectors set up by the students. Sid pulled up for a landing in front of the reactor chamber where his father and Dr. Macron were waiting. They helped them out of the jetpacks, and Talos transformed back into his hefty humanoid form and handed the control module to Dr. Macron.

Dr. Jamison herded everyone into the building, shouting, "Come on! Everybody inside!"

The asteroid was plainly visible now, glowing as it hit the atmosphere. Sid could see pieces breaking off—pieces the size of city blocks. Penny tugged at his arm. "Sid, we have to get inside!"

He tore his eyes from the asteroid and, for a second, cast his eyes out over the desolate Cretaceous landscape to where they had left the Alchemists. He followed Hari and Penny inside to the upper viewing gallery over the reactor. Image windows showed the scene outside Sci Hi. The shadow cast by the asteroid was getting darker as it got closer to Earth. Dr. Petraglif was at the controls, frantically recording data to study later—if there was a later.

Dr. Jamison's tense voice came over the intercom, "*The control module is in place. We're showing all green lights. Talos, it's up to you.*"

"*I am ready,*" the AI's calm voice answered. "*Ten seconds to jump.*"

Sid watched the asteroid as it closed in, and time seemed to slow down. Small chunks broke away from it, leaving a trail of smoke and dust as they encountered the atmosphere.

"Five seconds," said Talos.

The asteroid fell, streaking through the clouds.

"Impact," said Talos.

A pinpoint of brilliant light sparked to life, and the image window darkened to cut the glare. The space rock plowed right into the ground. In the first second, the six-mile-wide asteroid rammed into the Earth's surface, releasing the energy of hundreds of nuclear bombs. A tsunami of dirt and rock, melted by the massive energy released by the impact, splashed high up into the atmosphere. The light grew into an incandescent sphere as hot as the surface of the sun. The sphere expanded rapidly, vaporizing everything it touched.

Churchill felt the planet shake as the asteroid hit. He watched the wall of intense heat sweep inexorably toward them. *"NO!"* he roared. "The ancient alchemists did not predict this event! Man cannot know the workings of the universe without calling on the supernatural! They call themselves scientists…*hah*! They will never master this universe by watching and measuring. *Never*! *We* will prevail! We will rise and control the very engines of creation! We will…"

Churchill ranted until the heat vaporized him in a fraction of a second.

The blast reached the energy-collection grid, flooding it with power, and then destroying it in almost the same instant.

"Reactor power levels at 100 percent. Initiating time jump…now," Talos announced.

Sid watched, fear rising in his throat, as the shock wave of molten rock, uprooted trees, and dead creatures flew toward them. He closed his eyes reflexively, and his thoughts turned inside out.

When his head stopped spinning, he stood slowly, looking at the image being displayed on the huge video wall in awe.

Hari joined him. "I don't think we're home yet."

"Wow," Sid breathed in awe, "I have to go out and see this. Hey, Penny, wake up," He shook her arm.

Penny groggily climbed out of the chair she had collapsed into, and they made their way to a door, cracking the thick ice that had once again covered the entire island in a sparkling coat.

As Sid, Hari, and Penny crossed the campus toward an elevator station that would run down to the ground, they heard Dr. Macron's voice over the inter-island broadcasting system. *"Attention everyone! This is Dr. Macron. If you*

haven't already guessed, we were able to escape the Cretaceous period before the asteroid impact destroyed us. But we're not home yet. Unfortunately, we have jumped past our own time, and landed approximately 30 million years in the future.

"However, the reactor is in good shape, and thanks to the asteroid explosion, we have sufficient power to make the jump back to our home. It will take a few hours to get the reactor ready to make that last time jump. In the meantime, please stay inside. We'll sound an alert before the next time jump. Thank you."

"I don't know about this," Hari said. "Dr. Macron just said we should—"

Sidney's mental itch had him wild with curiosity. The idea of seeing the future—the *far* future—was just too irresistible. "Geez, Hari, has your brother Pradeep ever visited the future?" Sid said.

"Do you think you can get me to do anything just by saying that?" Hari demanded. He sighed in exasperation. "All right, let's go—but I'm going because I want to, not because of Pradeep, or *you*."

They descended to the ground and stepped out of the elevator.

"Amazing," Penny said softly.

They were standing on a flat expanse of soft, powdery sand. The sky was a dim reddish-purple as the sun set.

The full moon was a sullen red and much closer than Sid remembered.

In the distance, Sid saw some kinds of structures. They looked like buildings, but there was something wrong with them. They seemed to melt or dissolve, changing their shape as he watched. Spires formed and reached into the sky, only to run down and disappear. *It's like the buildings are alive*, he thought.

Small waves from the oily-looking ocean lapped at the shore, the water fizzing like soda. "Look at this," Hari said, stooping to pick up a shell. "I think it's some kind of sand dollar, but I've never seen one like this before." The corroded shell was flat, but instead of being round, it was hexagonal in shape. "It doesn't feel like a regular shell. It's made of some kind of metal, I think. Strange."

Penny looked around. "It's so quiet here." There were no sounds but the wind and the waves, no birds, or even bugs that she could see. The world was very different from the one they knew. "I wonder what happened? Could it... could it have been a mass extinction that wiped out...us?"

Hari shuddered. "That's a creepy thought." He looked around at the sand and rocks. "There's no sign of humans anywhere around here, is there?"

"Could have been a war, disease, something like that," Penny said. "Maybe another asteroid."

"If that's true, then the world's wide open again, isn't it?" Sid said. "I wonder what will inherit the Earth this time? Hey, look at that!" Sid pointed to a dog-size creature making its way along the shoreline. He had to wait until it was close enough to see through the mist. "It looks like some kind of beetle or something."

They walked over to the creature to get a better look. It looked a bit like a crab. Its pitted exoskeleton was a deep reddish gray with bright green and black markings. It had two pairs of walking limbs and three pairs of manipulator limbs. Two pairs had familiar-looking pincers, but the third set had a row of long spikes growing from it. The creature was using the spikes to sift through the sand, looking for something to eat. The four pincers occasionally picked up shells in the loosened sand for the creature to inspect closely with its eyestalks. Long antennae twitched in the ocean breeze. Occasionally, it fed a scrap of something into what must have been its mouth.

"That thing's freaky," Sid said, brushing at something tickling his cheek.

"That's not 'freaky,'" Penny said turning toward him, "it's actually quite—" She screamed in alarm, looking with panicked eyes over his shoulder.

Sid turned. The object tickling his cheek was the antenna of another crab creature, this one larger than a

person. Its forelimbs were twitching, as if it were just as surprised as Sidney.

Sid and Hari both yelped in surprise and rapidly backed away, but the creature didn't seem threatening. If anything, it seemed as surprised as they were.

"Hey, guys—I don't think if that thing's as alive as we think it is," Sid said. "Look at its joints. It looks like some kind of bot that got rusted in the water."

The creature's eyes telescoped out to peer more closely at Sid as he was talking.

"Okay, that's it. That thing is creeping me out," Penny said hurriedly. "Time to go back."

They ran back to the elevator, looking back occasionally to make sure the creature wasn't chasing them. Sid saw the huge robo-arthropod standing and watching them in the mist. It raised a claw, almost like it was waving to him. It looked disappointed somehow, he thought, like it would have liked to study him a bit more. Penny waved back at it.

Sid was lost in thought as they rode the elevator back up to the island.

"I don't know what happened here, but I'm ready to go home," Penny whispered.

Hari said thoughtfully, "It's like the world was taken over by robots or machines."

"I wonder if we caused our own extinction or if the machines caused it," Sid said.

As they walked back to the Tesla dorm building, the alert rang out.

"*Time jump in five minutes,*" a voice said. "*Prepare immediately.*"

Sid, Hari, and Penny sat down in a corner of the Tesla common room, along with the rest of their floor.

"*Time jump in ten seconds,*" the voice said.

Sid closed his eyes. *We have to make it this time*, he thought.

"*Time jump in three…two…one…*jump."

His thoughts twisted into impossible shapes as space-time folded around him.

CHAPTER 11

"All right, let's get started," The tall, well-dressed man stepped onto a podium that had been set up on the beach and spoke into a microphone.

"Hello, ladies and gentlemen, members of the press. We welcome you. My name is Alexander Ludd, and I represent the Alchemist Group, a think tank dedicated to putting a spotlight on deadly misuses of science and technology. I wish we were meeting under more fortunate circumstances, but this event symbolizes what we Alchemists have been warning the world about for centuries.

"The reason we're here today is to expose a great danger to you, to me, to all of us here in this nation and around the world. Most of you watching this press conference may not know that there has been an organization working in secret, hiding their schemes from the eyes of the world. Why? Why would a group of supposedly incorruptible people, *scientists*, be afraid of the spotlight of attention? Why do they hide?"

"Some people would say that the scientists of Goddard

Island are just avoiding the nuisance that the Alchemists are so good at creating," a reporter said, just loud enough to hear. There were a few chuckles from the crowd.

"Is it a nuisance," Ludd's voice boomed out, "to try to keep the world safe from people who would foolishly risk everything to carry out their deadly experimental programs? Yes, I said deadly! Man-made Goddard Island, which should have been standing just off the coast here," he gestured toward the ocean behind him, "has mysteriously disappeared…or been destroyed. Orbital satellites recorded a flash of light that was caused by a devastating explosion, vaporizing the island and everyone on it."

Reporters were glued to every word. News drones floated over the crowd, jostling each other for the best photo opportunity. Their turbofans competed to be heard with the crashing tide.

"The scientists on Goddard Island were engaged in reckless experimental activities that caused this horrible accident. This incident is a direct result of scientists meddling in processes they don't understand and can't control, without regard for the consequences.

"The Alchemists, on the other hand, have been safely studying the hidden mechanisms of the universe for thousands of years. We are on the verge of introducing a method of creating energy that will set us free from energy needs for the foreseeable—"

The speaker was interrupted by a flash of light on the surface of the ocean, about a quarter-mile from shore. A blast of cold air whipped through the crowd of spectators. Then, a sheet of water poured onto the shore, drenching everyone in chilly saltwater. The crowd shrieked and screamed in surprise and cold.

Alexander Ludd was knocked off the podium, and the sound system shorted out. He looked out over the ocean, and was hit by a wave of surprise and rage.

Goddard Island was back.

Sid, Hari and Penny stood in front of the Tesla dorm in the light of a rising sun. It looked to be early morning on a clear day.

The vision of the future Earth, without humans, filled Sid's mind. The Earth he had seen 30 million years in the future was disheartening and discouraging. All that humans had accomplished in their years on the planet had been swept away, leaving it open for...what? Cockroaches? Or possibly another species that, even now, possessed some spark of intelligence?

The good, the bad, the beautiful, and the ugliness that made humans human must have played a part in whatever destruction or catastrophe had ultimately happened.

Or might happen, Sid reminded himself. He frowned. The whole time travel thing was pretty confusing, and so much had happened, or was *going* to happen....

Penny said, "I don't know about you, but that future Earth looked kind of—I don't know, sad. It's pretty crazy to think that our world and all that humans have accomplished, could be swept away so completely. There didn't seem to be any traces, or at least any we could see from the beach."

Hari nodded, "It certainly makes you think, doesn't it? If those machines do end up eradicating human civilization, we've kind of done it to ourselves, haven't we?"

"Wait a second," Sid said. "From where we are now, the future hasn't happened yet. Could we...*change* the way the future unfolds? Maybe change the course of the river of time to arrive at a different destination?"

That thought cheered him. *Maybe we can do something to steer around the desolate, lonely world we glimpsed 30 million years into the future.*

"Maybe so," Hari agreed. "But for now, we have a bigger question to answer."

"Yeah. Are we home?" Penny asked nervously.

Hari studied the coastline through the heavy fog. "I'm not sure," he said.

They could hear a low thumping noise approaching.

Just then, Dr. Macron's voice rose from the outdoor speakers. *"Attention, everyone. I'm happy to report we're back in our own time! The last time jump was successful. Talos estimates that elapsed local time has only been twelve hours. Good work, everyone. We were successful in stopping the Alchemist plot to derail the work we're doing here on Goddard Island, and we'll make the authorities aware of what's happened. They won't dare to try anything, at least for a while. But if they do, we'll be on guard for any future attempts at terrorism and disinformation.*

We're setting up disinfection stations outside the dorms and at other locations around the island to kill any bacteria we might have brought back with us. Make sure you check in via your voxpods when you're through. Welcome home, everybody!"

Sid could hear the cheers that rang out across the island. Score one for Sci Hi! Sidney wasn't going to be satisfied until every Alchemist was discredited, but at least there were three less around to destroy scientific progress—and his family.

A crowd formed on the lawn as scientists and students rushed out to admire the ocean landscape they knew and loved. When he spotted Dr. Petraglif, she gave him a wink. This time, Sidney winked back.

A group of helicopters broke through the morning mist, approaching the island and landing in an open area. Military personnel emerged first, followed by civilians. Sid recognized one of them.

"*Mom!*" he yelled, but he was still too far away. "C'mon, you guys!" He started running toward the helicopters, followed by Penny, Hari, and the rest of the students as they raced to meet their families.

"Sidney!" his mother called out once she spotted him. "Thank goodness you're all right!" She gave him a fierce hug. "I thought you...all of you...were gone, or worse." She pulled away, eyes welling up with emotion. "What happened to the island?"

"It's kind of a long story, Mom, but basically—" Sid began, but someone interrupted him.

"Ellen?" Sid's father said.

Mrs. Jamison looked blankly at a person for whom she had long since given up hope. Her mouth opened a couple of times with no sound as she slowly walked to her long-lost husband.

"Rob? *Rob*, is that really you? "You've been gone for *so long*! What happened to you? Are you...are you all right?" She gingerly touched his face, and then they hugged tightly.

"Yeah, a few hundred million years," Sid's dad chuckled. "It's a bit of a story. But with Sid's help, I made it back in one piece." He glanced at his left wrist. "Well, except for the watch you gave me for our anniversary. I lost it somewhere in the Triassic, unfortunately."

Mrs. Jamison laughed as tears ran down her cheeks, "The watch!" She tried to say something, but she was too overcome to get it out. She looked at Sidney.

"Oh, yeah!" Sid said, digging into one of his pants cargo pockets. "I have the watch here. Mom gave it to me." He held it out to his father. "This wouldn't happen to be yours, would it?" He handed his father the resin casting of the flattened watch. "It's pretty beat up, and there's 200-million-year-old bug guts on it."

"Wow, Sid, it is. I can see a tiny bit of engraving on the back," his father said. "How did you find it?"

"I think the time jump effect is...elastic in some way, and the watch was snapped back to our time," Sid said, shrugging.

"That watch was the only evidence that you had even been in the reactor chamber that night," Sid's mom smiled.

Sid was about to launch into the story of what had happened to them during their disappearance, but Penny tapped him on the shoulder. There were two adults behind her.

"Sorry to interrupt, Sidney, but I want you to meet my parents," she said. Everyone shook hands all around and started talking. Sid looked around the campus to see a giant party was taking place. Robots were bringing out food and drinks, and everyone was laughing and smiling.

Sid spotted Hari with a few people. "Hey, there's Hari. That must be his parents he's talking to. And that has *got* to be the infamous Pradeep."

"We simply have to meet him," Penny grinned.

They slipped away from their parents and approached Hari and his family.

"Yeah, I want to see Pradeep's face when he gets the download on what Hari's been up to," Sid said.

When they joined Hari's parents, they were telling Hari about how wonderfully Pradeep was doing, learning the family business. Pradeep, a rather pudgy young man with slightly protruding eyeballs, was chewing on a sandwich and looking down his nose at Hari.

Sid and Penny stood slightly behind Hari, waiting for a break in the Pradeepian praise to introduce themselves. It never came.

Hari finally broke into his mother's lengthy diatribe of Pradeep's most recent successes, slamming his nanobot trophy in Pradeep's face.

"What's that? Pradeep asked. "I don't see anything,"

"Exactly!" Hari remarked bitterly.

"You're blind to Hari's talents!" Penny exclaimed. "He's smart, kind, and courageous."

"Yeah, and he's lethally competetive," Sid said ruefully.

"Meet Penny and Sidney," Hari said. "They're my friends. They're going to be scientists, like me."

Pradeep's eyeballs looked like they were going to pop out of his head. Evidently, no one had ever interrupted a listing of Pradeep's glowing qualities before now. The Guptas stared at Hari as if they had never met him, and Sid could see something resembling respect in their eyes.

"Let's go," Hari said, storming off.

"Um, nice to meet you," Sid said, throwing Hari's family a wave as he and Penny ran to catch up to Hari.

"You can hang out with our families, Hari," Penny said, throwing an arm over his shoulders.

"Yeah," Sid agreed. "I didn't really believe you when you went on about how Pradeep was the golden child in your family. Wow. I felt sick just watching that."

"Actually," Hari grinned, "I feel better than I have in a long time!"

They crossed the grass to where Sid and Penny's families were talking animatedly. The friends joined in.

"It was an amazing adventure," Penny said. "I'll have enough extinct species to draw for the rest of my life. My illustrations are going to be famous! What an art exhibition.

Never before seen by human eyes! I'm the only person on Earth who can paint dinosaurs in their *true colors*. Can't top that! It'll be brilliant!"

"We'll help you set it up," Hari said. "I want to design a robot that can go back to all those different time periods and really spend time exploring, the same way we've sent robot probes out to Mars, Venus, and Jupiter's moons. Can you imagine the things we would be able to learn?"

"I'm going to take down the Alchemists." Sid said. "The only way to avoid the future we saw is with science and leaving behind the kind of supernatural nonsense they're peddling. I feel like that's what I'm meant to do, and the tools we're learning to use here at Sci Hi are the way to do it."

"That's going to be a big job, don't you think?" Penny asked.

"The biggest," Sid said, grinning, "but I feel like I'm in the right place at the right time to do it—if you know what I mean!"

TIME JUMP

Reader's Guide

What Do YOU Think?

Scientists ask a lot of questions—questions with many different answers. There are no right or wrong answers to these questions about *Time Jump*. But a good Sci Hi student knows the best answers are those that are supported by evidence!

 At first, Sidney isn't much interested in history, especially prehistory. He prefers things he can see and touch to investigate. Do you share Sidney's view on the past? Why or why not?

 When the Goddard Island crew discovers Sidney's dad Rob, they take him back to the present, which is actually the future for Rob. What do you think of their decision? Would you have made the same one?

 Hari feels a lot of pressure to measure up to his older brother, Pradeep. How does this sibling rivalry impact Hari's choices? Can you think of examples when this influence is positive, negative, or both?

 Drawing is Penny's favorite pastime, but it also frustrates her when she doesn't do it perfectly. Do you have a hobby that you love that you wish you were better at? Does the advice Rob gives Penny apply to you?

The students have different views on the effects of time travel on the present. Do you share Sid's worries about changing the future, or do you buy into Hari's belief that time can flow around an event?

The watch Rob was wearing when he time-jumped snapped back to the present. If this elastic bounce-back effect left evidence of Goddard Island in the past, how could it affect the present they returned to?

Dr. Petraglif names the cloned Metoposaurus "Fluffy," as if the amphibian were a dog or a cat. Would any of the prehistoric creatures the Sci Hi students see make a good family pet? Why or why not?

Rob survived the Triassic for many months by dining on bugs, fish, and leftover meat scraps. If you were stranded in prehistory, where would you look for food? Are there things you simply wouldn't eat?

The Science of Sci Hi

Many of the science-fiction elements in *Time Jump* are inspired by real scientific theory. Read on to discover the fascinating facts behind the fiction!

Time Travel

Most physicists agree that time travel is possible. Time slows around objects accelerating through space, meaning that they are traveling faster than time. Someone (or something) could travel to the future in this way. But an important scientific rule is that cause comes before effect. That rule would make it impossible for us to travel to the past, where events have already solidified.

Prehistoric Clones

Scientists have made major breakthroughs in DNA research—decoding our makeup and even cloning animals. But DNA strands deteriorate quickly, making it unrealistic to clone a prehistoric beast. Still, we might be able to create a dino-like creature by manipulating the genes of a dinosaur descendant, such as a chicken, by turning or off certain characteristics to roll back evolution.

Fossilization

Bones turn to dust quickly—it doesn't even take 100 years! So how can we uncover the skeleton of a dinosaur millions of years after it lived? Sometimes, when material is buried in sand or mud, intense pressure preserves the item. Minerals seep into the pores (or small holes) in the organic, or living, matter, gradually replacing what was there before. The end result is a stone replica. So, the dinosaur skeletons we see in museums are actually stone, not bone.

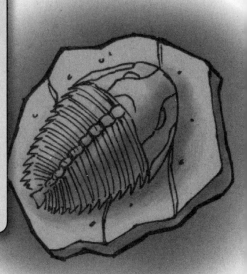

Climate Change

A massive asteroid was the beginning of the end of the Cretaceous period. The climate change it caused resulted in the biggest mass extinction our world has known. But there were prior prehistoric mass extinctions, too. They started out differently, but in each case, climate change impacted life on our planet. That has many scientists worried about the effect global warming might have on our future.

Prehistoric Timeline

The Permian Period

Years: 290–248 million years ago

Description: Amphibians are emerging and early reptiles have appeared, but protomammals rule in this swampy forest atmosphere. Pangea is one complete continent.

Known for: Protomammals are the dominant life form. Tusked herbivores live alongside long-toothed, doglike predators. At the end, mass extinction wipes out 70 percent of land animals and 96 percent of sea life. *Lystosaurus* is one of the few to survive.

The Triassic Period

Years: 248–205 million years ago

Description: Reptiles begin their reign! The ancestors of the crocodile are large and in charge in this desolate environment, caused by volcano eruptions and greenhouse effects. It's incredibly hot.

Known for: Reptiles, including the first dinosaurs, dominate a landscape with hardly a fern where lush forests once stood. At the end of this period, Pangea begins to break apart, separating animals and ecosystems.

The Jurassic Period

Years: 205–138 million years ago

Description: Just as life begins to flourish again in the Triassic, another mass extinction brings on the Jurassic. Half the life on the planet won't live to experience the new era, but the dinosaurs survive and thus begin their rule.

Known for: Dinosaur domination begins as these reptiles fill the space the extinct species left behind. They become much larger over this period, and many new (and sometimes strange) species evolve as Pangea's continents continue to drift and shift.

The Cretaceous Period

Years: 138–63 million years ago

Description: The Earth begins to look more familiar and modern, with the continents as we know them taking shape. Mammals are mostly small and in hiding, and the dinosaurs continue to rule the land.

Known for: Separate land masses allow many new species to develop. Pterosaurs fly overhead, gigantic beasts of all shapes cover the land, and marine animals larger than whales swim in the water. It's a reptile paradise until disaster strikes.

Would You Survive Prehistory?

Rob survives the Triassic by relying on his wits. Test your survival knowledge with this quick quiz.

1. There's no grocery store or restaurant nearby. You have to eat. Which do you choose?

   A I don't see any fruit yet, but I'll keep looking—how long could it take?

   B Sauropods eat 1,000 pounds of trees a day—how bad can they be?

   C Slimy insects will slide down the gullet—but will they come back up?

2. You're exhausted. You know you have to sleep, but the question is where—and when?

   A I'll just keep walking until I find a nice, soft, mossy surface or a bed of ferns.

   B I'm going to take a cue from the other mammals and find a nighttime nook.

   C There's nothing like a nap in the sun—I'll climb a tree and sleep through the day.

3. Water, water, everywhere—but what is safe to drink?

   A I'll stick to the rainwater, thanks. I'm sure I can collect it with some leaves.

   B There aren't pollutants in prehistory, so the animals' watering holes are safe.

   C I don't trust any of the water in this place—I'll just get my fluid from foods.

4. What's the safest way to spend your days?

   A I will get the most incredible tan of my lifetime basking in the sun.

   B I think I'll stick to the shade and maybe pile up some rocks for safety.

   C It's important to keep moving—I'm sure I'll find shelter if I need it.

Answers

1. Gross as it is, the answer is C. There are no fruit trees in the Triassic, and we humans can't digest fiber like dinosaurs, so trees wouldn't provide enough nutrients.

2. You would be a smart mammal if you answered B. A lot of hunting likely took place at night, the prehistoric sun would scorch you as you slept, and ferns were scarce.

3. To survive, A is the answer. Water bodies would be full of organisms that could make you ill. And you would survive longer without food than water.

4. If you answered B, you're a survivor. In that desolate space, you could run miles before stumbling upon a natural shelter. You would also need protection from the Triassic sun and "wildlife."

Superlative Beasts

Whose the fairest of them all? Dinos didn't have to worry about who was the prettiest. But it definitely mattered who was the strongest! Check out some of history's most amazing dinos below!

Smallest dinosaur

Compsognathus was believed to be the smallest—until paleontologists discovered their sample was a juvenile. Now *Microraptor*—a dinosaur with four wings, a 15" fast-runner named *Parvicursor*, and the feathered and beaked *Caenagnathasia* vie for the recognition.

Biggest dinosaur

At 65 feet tall, 130 feet long, and weighing in at around 70 tons, *Argentinosaurus* should easily hold this title. But a yet-to-be-named 2014 discovery from Argentina may displace the current champ. Both gigantic sauropods are members of the subgroup *Titanosaurs*.

Fastest dinosaur

As with the other superlatives, it's hard to award this title to just one winner. There are a whole group of super speedy *ornithomimids*—a mouthful of a word used to describe ostrich-like dinosaurs. They had long limbs and light frames, and evidence suggests that they could sprint at speeds of at least 25 miles per hour.

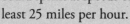

Fiercest dinosaur

Think it's *T. rex*? Think again. *P. rex* is smaller but quicker and perhaps deadlier! The *P* stands for "Pinocchio", and though the name is laughable, its longer snout and powerful jaws came along with an extra helping of stealth. And don't count out *Spinosaurus*—the African beast with a crocodile-like jaw and formidable size.

Smartest dinosaur

Dinosaurs have gotten a bad rap in terms of intelligence, but now we believe they were actually quite smart for reptiles. *T. rex* had a brain about the size of ours, which is impressive until you consider how big the body was! *Troodon* was about our size, though, and it had the brain the size of a golf ball. If you're measuring by brain size to body size, that makes it not only the smartest dino but also the smartest Mesozoic animal.

Choose Your Battle-Bot

"Sleek and speedy" has its advantage, as does "thick and sturdy." What kind of nanobot would you design to take into a competition?

When it comes to body shape …

A bigger is always the best option

B small size has its advantages

C short but thick is the way to go

The most effective weaponry is powered by …

A pistons

B electricity

C magnetism

Your signature move would be …

A mighty strong punches

B whiplike speed and accuracy

C energetic pushing power

Which is most important to you?

A muscling through obstacles

B lightning-quick reflexes

C stability and staying power

Your bot's style influence is …

A cartoons and comics

B art and sculpture

C mechanics and engineering

Which bot did you choose?

If you answered mostly *A*s, you chose Sid's bot. The Crusher is stout and stable, and he can smash opponents into smithereens with his bulk and pounding power.

If you answered mostly *B*s, you chose Penny's bot. Medusa is slim, sleek, and refined, but her speed and electric filament whips make this beauty lethal.

If you answered mostly *C*s, you chose Hari's bot. Jack the Gripper is a true terror with his hard-to-hit stature and magnetic ability to make metal a weapon.

Craft a Prehistoric Pet

Dinosaur bones turn to stones, so why not reverse-engineer a regular rock into a prehistoric pet?

What You'll Need

- A rock—any size, any material, but the bumpier the better

- Feathers, now known to be an absolute essential for dinos

- Fabric, googly eyes, and other craft materials to decorate

- Craft glue, of course, to make all those fun features stick

What You'll Do

1. Examine your rock. Are there bumps that look like horns? Divots that would make good eye sockets? Decide what kind of beast your rock wants to become.

2. Place the face first. Add googly eyes, or paint the eyes in place. An egg carton or cardstock will shape a nice snout. Paper plates can be cut into solid-looking teeth.

3. Give your pet pizzazz. Dinos were the most decorative creatures to ever walk the Earth. They had spines, spikes, horns, claws, and tails. Let your imagination go wild!

4. Add feathers. Maybe your rock pet is covered in feathers, or maybe they appear just around its pom-pon feet or neck. There's no wrong way to feather your beast.

5. Name your pet. Prehistoric pets without names are statistically more likely to eat their owners. Don't be a statistic, not after you've learned to survive the Triassic!

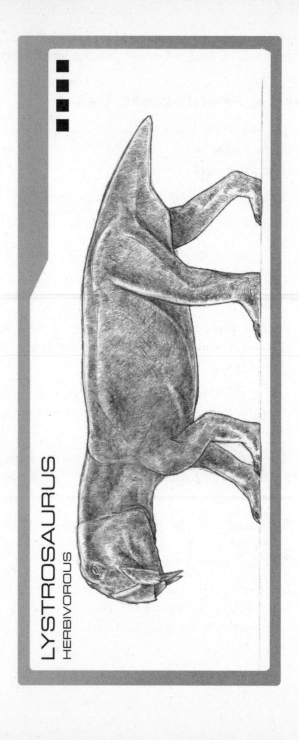

LYSTROSAURUS
HERBIVOROUS

TANYSTROPHEUS
CARNIVOROUS

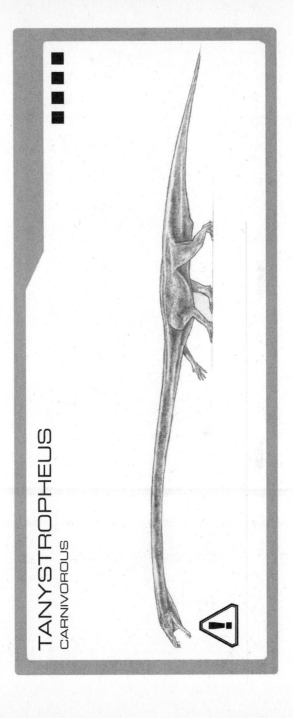

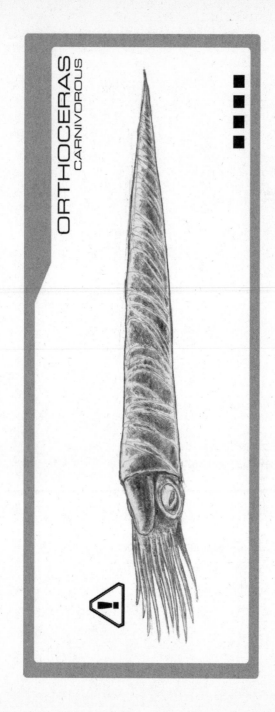

ORTHOCERAS
CARNIVOROUS

NANOBOT
TROPHY

MAGNIFIED 1,000,000 TIMES